THE SUFFERING

THE SUFFERING was originally published under the pseudonym Amy Abelli under the title *The Girlfriend*. It won a Honourable Mention at the 2015 San Francisco Book Festival for Best Gay Fiction. It has been made into a French-language feature film, *La Souffrance,* starring Roxanne Fernandes.

THE SUFFERING

THE SUFFERING

Lighthouse

Lake Ozark Press

Copyright © 2015 Laurent Boulanger

Lighthouse is an imprint of Lake Ozark Press, Missouri, USA

Typeset in Garamond

Cover design © 2015 Lake Ozark Press

For those who have loved, lost and survived.

And for those who have loved, lost and never recovered

THE SUFFERING

CHAPTER ONE

In the twenty-second year of her life Amelia is playing tennis alone against a faded terracotta brick wall. She wears a yellow, cotton tennis top, a blue, cotton short and white tennis shoes. She is pretty with short, brown hair, but not necessarily in a conventional way. Her skin is a little pale for someone who plays sport outdoors, but it's something that's been running in her family. The French in her is Norman, and the Normans have ancestry in Great Britain, where the sun is not particularly nourishing to the complexion of its people. Her eyes are hazel, but they metamorphose to a pale green in summer. She has a button nose and freckles, which makes her look much younger than she is. When she goes clubbing, the doormen always ask for identification because they never believe she is over eighteen years of age. There are advantages in looking much younger than you really are; the main one being you end up bedding younger lovers—girls with soft, bubble-gum-smelling skin wrapped in thin, bony frames and big, alarmed eyes made even larger with black mascara and eye liner. You can also buy cinema tickets and enter other places at a lower price of admission if the ticket seller believes you are anywhere between fourteen and seventeen.

Amelia focuses and hits the ball hard, almost in anger. Her

face is covered in sweat, and her muscles are tensed in an effort not to miss the ball. She hits the ball back-and-forth for over a minute, relentlessly running from one side of the court to the other. The adrenalin rush is exactly what she needs, something she can never get by sitting around at home or watching the ocean for hours by sitting at the far end of a pier. She doesn't really like sport, but she forces herself to do exercises because it makes a feel a little more grounded, not as if she is walking on clouds all the time.

If a stranger suddenly stopped to watch her, he would notice she is slender and has a tired look about her, as if she hasn't had a good night's sleep for at least a month. She doesn't have a friend to play tennis with. She doesn't have a regular day job, or she wouldn't be playing tennis early afternoon on a weekday.

It's a sunny day without a cloud in sight. The park is almost deserted like it always is early Tuesday afternoons. There's traffic in the near-distance from the highway, which runs along-side the beach toward Port Melbourne, half a kilometre south, and a man walking a small white and brown dog— maybe a Jack Russell, but she can't be certain—along the edge of the north end of the park, past the football oval, not far from the back entrance of the local Woolworths supermarket. It smells of spring flowers and sea salt. The sound of birds singing from elms fills the air like lovers who believe they have all the time in the world.

Eventually Amelia misses hitting back the ball, and it bounces off in the distance, across the road and vanishes somewhere in the grass near a tall red gum eucalyptus, which has stood still for at least four-hundred years. Frustration takes over her. Without a second thought, she gives up and sits down against the hardness of the grey bitumen, the little loose stones poking at her bum cheeks like pieces of glass from a broken bottle, the slight discomfort somehow comforting in the oddest way.

She thinks about Jasmine, who has left her suddenly without any warning, the way a selfish owner abandons a pet by the side of the road the morning of a getaway summer vacation. Love is the cruellest of all emotions because it takes hold of you without warning, makes you believe in security and some life purpose when everything seems meaningless, but then it turns on you, rejects you, screams you are not worthy, lets you simmer in your own loneliness and pathetic decay.

That was three weeks ago, but Amelia is still hurting as if it had all happened only this morning—the wounds raw on the inside even though there is no scaring on the outside.

Almost in tears now, Amelia closes her eyes and feels the texture of Jasmine's skin against the palm of her hand and the tips of her fingers, the bitter-sweet taste of her sex on her tongue, the smell of her white musk perfume in the air. It is as if Jasmine is still next to her, breathing the same air, playing tennis like they used to twice a week at the Peanut Farm Reserve.

Not long ago Jasmine and Amelia shared a two-bedroom, ground-floor apartment in Mitford Street, only a few minutes walking distance from the park. They used to catch tram 96 together to get to the city centre, and in winter they took long walks down the Esplanade and the adjoining beach, walked up the pier and shared hot chocolates at the Little Blue restaurant, which sits neatly behind the St Kilda Pier Kiosk at the edge of the water, one-hundred-and-fifty meters from the coastline.

When Jasmine disappeared, Amelia moved into a large three-bedroom apartment on Alma Road in a quiet Jewish neighbourhood, a world away from the bohemian lifestyle of Acland and Fitzroy Streets. She can't really afford the rent by herself, but she believes Jasmine will be back soon and will share the cost of the lease, the food and the utilities. Walking to her new apartment from the Peanut Farm Reserve after a solo game of tennis is too far, so she bought herself a yellow convertible, a second-hand Mietta she saw for sale on Ebay. She bought it with her credit card, a silly thing to do because she knows with her job, there is no guarantee she'll be able to make the repayments.

An impulse buy.

One of the many impulse buys she's allowed herself to indulge in since life became an fire-storm of confusing and confronting emotions.

A gift to herself to overcome the vanishing of Jasmine from her life.

Half an hour later she is back home under a steaming shower, masturbating vigorously with the imaginary presence of Jasmine assaulting her five senses. It is as if Jasmine is right there with her. They have taken many showers together, and if she closes her eyes, she can still feel Jasmine's presence in the room like a ghost who refuses to leave for heaven and instead chooses to remain in purgatory. Jasmine's fingers are digging inside her, she makes herself believe, when in reality it's her own fingers.

The bathroom is white and everything seems to be clinically clean other than her sweaty tennis gear lying on the tiled floor —her yellow top, blue dress, white panties, pink socks, white shoes—what she wore this morning when playing tennis. The sound of the shower run-ning is drilling in the confinement of the small apartment, like thumb pins thrown against a window pane.

The glass enclosure is fogged with steam, her back almost red-raw from the hot water. There's a black-ink tattoo down half the length of her spine in Chinese characters, which look like the root of a tree climbing down from her skull. It reads *that which feeds me also destroys me.* She believes the philosophical statement is a true representation of her personality, of what has to deal with in life, whether it be love or addiction or anything in between.

She is now breathing heavily and eventually grunting. Her fingers are squeezing her clitoris and then rubbing it. She does this too roughly—and she knows it—but the thought of having Jasmine with her in the shower is too much excitement to contain. She never anticipated she would resort to masturbation on a daily basis, but it calms her down and gives her some sense of control over her sexual frustration and her unbearable state of existence.

Amelia turns the shower off with her free hand.

The shower trickles, and she finally stops and presses her face against the smoked shower glass, satisfied but disgusted with herself all at once. She brings her fingers to her nostrils and smells her own sex, fantasising it to be Jasmine's. But it only lasts a few seconds because every woman has her own particular odour, and this is not the taste of Jasmine she took into her mouth on a daily basis.

She wants to believe the masturbation ses-sions are only temporary, and Jasmine will be back soon.

Amelia steps out of the shower exhausted from the tennis game and the masturbation, her brain filled with endorphins, the same effect those anti-depressants have on her. This reminds her she's nearly out of Xanax, and she'll have to go back to her psychiatrist to get a refill. She doesn't like going much because the doctor is male and too intrusive. She's never been able to relate to men, or to women who like men. She never liked dick, and she never will, no matter how much her father thinks it's just a phase she's going through. She hasn't dared to tell him, but she often thought of asking him if he ever woke up in the middle of the night with penis envy—*see how you like it.*

A few minutes later, Amelia is in front of the mirror, a pink towel wrapped around her body. She applies moisturiser to her face. She does this slowly, like she's got all the time in the world—and she does. She slicks her dark hair back with a blue plastic comb. Her hair is short, too short maybe, maybe too

5

obvious she likes girls, and it bothers her a little because she knows how people judge you and everything you do and say just because of your sexual preference.

She checks herself left and then right.

She doesn't seem happy or unhappy, just going through the daily motions.

What business is it to the world what I do with my pussy?

It's a small, dark and poorly furnished apart-ment, which smells of white mould and deca-ying brickwork. She picked up most of the furniture from side-walks—couches, tables, chairs, beds, mattresses, lamps, toasters, heaters, all discarded by young people who have moved on in life and left the inner suburbs in order to afford their first home some thirty kilometres away in a new housing estate, which used to be swamp and dried- out shrubs only a decade ago. The white-washed walls of her bedroom are blank, apart from a silver-framed print of some sort with a half-naked girl done in charcoal Amelia found tossed next to a rubbish bin. Her breasts are fully exposed, but her pubic region is covered with white panties—sometimes imagination is better than reality.

It's a young woman's place, one who does not have much money, like the hundred thousands who finish school or university every year and need to make their way into the independent lives of adults, filled with its financial and moral obligations, demands that can come as a shock for those who have been sheltered by their parents for the first two decades of their lives—this new life is like a car crash along a desolated country road stretch on a quiet Sunday morning.

She works as a model, but the work is irregular, and it's a typical fast-or-famine cycle when working under contract without any form of security. Once a week, she shoplifts at the local supermarket because groceries and toiletries are so expensive she cannot afford them. Survival extinct. It's human nature. If the world doesn't supply you with the necessities of life, you have to get them yourself, no matter what the cost, no matter how dishonest it might be. She doesn't question much any more—she is a shoplifter, and she knows it. If she had money, she wouldn't be doing it, so she knows it's a money issue and not because she's a kleptomaniac. The whole process is stressful and annoying and forces her to be who she is not. You need to be a criminal just to survive these days because past generations think suffering and poverty builds character in the same way education opens doors to unforesee-able possibilities.

There is no safe income in modelling, not when you haven't made it big yet. She knows because her father keeps on reminding her every time he comes to visit. In a way, she knows she's not totally at fault—a product of her generation where everyone is a star or an artist struggling to unchain themselves from a suffocating cocoon of tradition and money-focused careers. She could have worked in a shop or in a bank or even enrolled at law school when she was accepted a couple of years ago. God only knows how she managed to get admitted in the first place because she never studied. She was blessed with a photographic memory, so it was easy for her to remember details, dates and events even if she had only read once about them. Her weakness was argument and debate, something she would have to work on if she wanted a career as a lawyer or a solicitor.

A career.

Modern, legal slavery.

But her father will remind her soon enough how it's the same for the rest of the world, and soon she'll have to come back to her senses and realise she is just another part of the mysterious puzzle of life. She already dreads the next time he is going to come to visit and ask her all kind of questions about what she is eating, whom she is seeing, when is she going to come back to her senses and return to study. She is fighting the fight every single generation has to fight—rich or poor, black or white, man or woman. The only way to become the person you want to be is to fiercely deny the needs of your parents, their plan they built from the day you were born until the day you leave the nest. And even after you've left the nest, the nagging and power struggle continues, the constant need to control someone else's life. She knows some of the most successful people had the worst child-hoods, the least supporting parents and the hardest time adjusting to what society expected from them. On the surface, and to her friends, she seems adjusted—but appearances can be as deceptive as white lies.

Amelia is lying on the single bed, dressed in nothing but her white panties. She doesn't wear a bra. The shape of her nipples are perfectly symmetric, brown aureoles, almost chocolate in colour. She likes them. They are just the right size. Jasmine told her. The darkness of her bush is a shadow against the whiteness of her panties. She looks up to the ceiling—she seems bored, maybe even confused. The room smells enclosed and musky, which doesn't help her state of despair.

The television is on in the background, but she is not watching. A man and a woman are arguing about how love doesn't last and there is no such thing anyway. She agrees in her mind but refuses to accept it at face-value.

She turns to the right, and next to her are a bunch of prescription pills in small orange vials. Her name is clearly printed on one of the vials: AMELIA LOCKHART.

There's also a clock radio that reads 2.17 a.m.

She takes one of the vials, opens it and pops a couple of pills in her mouth. She washes the pills down with a mouthful of water from a plastic bottle next to the bed. The water is lukewarm, but she doesn't mind because cold water gives her a sore throat.

When she is done, she puts the bottle down and goes back to lying down on the bed.

Time goes slowly, but with a stomach filled with pills, it's never as painful—there is relief and a sense of careless detachment about life when your mind is simmering in a cocktail of chemicals designed to stop you going crazy from your own thoughts. She doesn't know how she can manage to survive on so little sleep, but at night things always seem worse.

Soon the morning light will come like a slap in the face, and some newly-found courage will carry her through the burden of her existence for another loveless and meaningless day.

CHAPTER TWO

It's evening, and Amelia is sitting at the kitchen table, a plate full of food in front of her—chicken and potatoes, and carrots, peas and cauliflower from a frozen pack. She never buys fresh vegetables because they go off before she gets time to eat them—and they are also more expensive than frozen vegetables.

She bought the kitchen table on Ebay, a Formica-like white top with galvanised legs, the type popular in the 1960s or 1970s. Her grandmother and uncle used to have similar ones, and whilst she didn't think much of them at the time, it now brings her comfort, like an old friend who has been around for years, someone you can depend on, even when life throws a hurricane in your path.

The kitchen is clean and everything is in its place, but it's because she's got too much free time on her hands, not because she's an obsessive cleaner. She never knows when her father is going to drop in for a visit, so it is obligatory to keep the apartment as neat as possible. He is a typical parent, and whilst he means well, he can be quite careless when commenting on her life.

There are six yellow mugs sitting under the window sill, two yellow dishcloths hanging over the oven, a yellow toaster on the bench with a yellow water jug next to it. All this yellow should make her happy, but it doesn't, and she knows now you can't really colour your life in shades of happiness with no one around you. It's like being a blind person who struggles to work on a watercolour by fingering the paint and smudging it on the canvas in hope something meaningful and artistic will result.

She wears a red, cotton dress with white polka dots, and her make-up is beautifully applied in a natural look, which is much harder to achieve than it would appear for those who know little about make-up. She knows beauty is constructed, and she's become a master at it.

There's another plate filled with food opposite hers—chicken, potatoes, carrots, peas—but there is no one sitting there, only an empty chair, like a person lost at sea waiting for someone to find her.

She is waiting for Jasmine. It's not polite to eat from your plate until everyone is at the dinner table. Her father drilled table manners into her since the day she could make senses of what was going on in the world.

Footsteps echo in the confinement of the apartment block.

Someone is getting close to her front door.

She looks up, a glint of hope on her face.

Jasmine?

Then the footsteps vanish, and another door is being shut somewhere else in the building.

A neighbour.

There's disappointment on Amelia's face, as if someone has just told her she's got six months to live. The pins in her stomach are ripping her apart, and she wishes she could put an end to all the pain—*right now!*

That same night, in the confinement of the bathroom, Amelia can't take it anymore.

She is sitting naked against the white bathtub, her head

down. She focuses on her task, her rib cage clearly visible through the thin layer of white skin that miraculously holds it all together. The bone-coloured tiles are cold underneath her bare feet because the bathroom window doesn't shut properly and cold air is a permanent fixture. She should be dressed, but it's much more dramatic to be naked when self-mutilating. In her mind's eye, she sees her life as a movie, as if someone out there is watching her every move. Reality television has corrupted her mind like those of a whole generation who believe there are hidden cameras everywhere, and they are the stars of the show. She is totally absorbed in her task, like a surgeon removing stitches—except in this case she is the reason why stitches will be required some day. Cuts upon cuts means the wounds are not healing as well as they should, and the scars are turning into their own version of a tattoo drawn with blood, not ink.

With a small, silver nail file, she scratches her left wrist, not deep enough to cut, but deep enough to leave marks. She is getting off on it but not in a major way—just as a form of relief. There are almost tears in her eyes as she wonders what she is doing here alone in the room, in the apartment, in this world. Is it the same for everyone else? Or is this loneliness some kind of punishment she deserves for karmic reasons, or because she's incapable of letting go of the past and moving on with her life?

She has no answer because she is too young, and youth is filled with endless possibilities but no wisdom.

When done, she puts the nail file away, and then she retrieves some antiseptic from the bathroom cabinet. She applies it on a cotton make-up pad and washes the scratches. She's doing this very systematically, like she's done a hundred times before. The cold air coming from the bathroom window is making her shiver now, and she notices the goosebumps on her skinny arms. She almost loves being this weak because it excuses her from having the willpower to be strong.

Depression is as addictive as caffeine—an abuser who makes you feel your existence is meant to be an expression of suffering.

The smell of antiseptic is like being in a hospital—clinically comforting even if a little nauseous.

When done with the cutting, she applies a couple of flesh-coloured adhesive bandages to the scratches. The bandages feel like a second skin covering the damage she has caused. No one will really know, but those who are also self-harming will recognise the signs of anguish and desperation.

When done, she places the antiseptic and make-up pads in the bathroom cabinet.

She checks herself in the mirror—her hazel eyes void of any detectable emotions—and leaves the bathroom.

In the corner of her bedroom, Amelia is sitting on a wooden chair and is painting her toe nails blood red—cottons balls between her toes. She focuses on her task, as if it is the most important thing in the world. The odour of vanish is strong, but she likes it—a bit like the little glue sticks she used to sniff with Jasmine behind the bicycle shed, back at high school.

The room is bright and sunny, but her mind is filled with darkness like an everlasting winter.

Amelia is plucking her eyebrows in the bathroom, the pain annoying but comforting all at once.

When she is done, she checks herself in the mirror, and it's hard to tell if she is happy or unhappy with the result. She thinks the arches don't match, but to a passer-by they would seem just perfect.

She doesn't feel perfect.

She knows she never will.

It's after lunch and Amelia is sitting at the kitchen table, her notebook opened in front of her, her smart-phone and a mug of coffee next to it. The smell of coffee is strong because she'd only just made a pot, and she'll be drinking from it for the rest of the day. She hasn't slept well last night, but she doesn't like sleeping during the day because it keeps her awake at all hours.

The kitchen is clean, but not as clean as when she had dinner the other night. The bin needs emptying, and there is a plastic bottle of diet cola lying next to it. A saucer and small plate are waiting their turn in the sink.

Amelia is looking with great concentration at the screen of her notebook. She reads, a serious look on her face, and then she types furiously. Her expression then relaxes as she reads.

She frowns and she types again with great concentration. She stops and reads from the screen. The world around her doesn't exist when she is on Facebook. The social network program is both a blessing and nuisance. She knows the hours she spends on it could be spent doing something more productive, but other than modelling, she's not much good at anything. Some of her friends write, some play music, some paint—she has no real talent she can use to occupy all those lonely hours. With Jasmine, she didn't need any talent because someone else's company is an enjoyable time-filler itself.

Her smart-phone vibrates on the tabletop.

She picks it up and checks the message that has just come through. A spam message. She gets more and more these days, and she has no idea how they got her cell phone number. She chooses to ignore it and puts the phone down again.

She takes a sip from her coffee mug and continues to read the screen. She puts the coffee down and types quickly with obsessive concentration, like the way people do on their smart-phones when waiting for a bus or during their lunch-break—united but separated all at once. She has no idea what people used to do before the Internet existed, and whilst she's actually aware she's from a generation blessed with digital communication, she doesn't fully comprehend how people from the past filled long, empty hours.

14

Amelia is lying in bed wearing only a pair of white panties and a grey cotton tee-shirt. She's reading a second-paper copy of an old book from the the nineteen-forties about some guy who travels all over America with nothing in mind but the hope of finding oneself and becoming a writer.

She stops reading and looks towards her desk. There's a photo of Jasmine smiling at her, a notebook, some fashion magazines—with her face on one of the covers—a half-burnt candle, a jewellery box with jewellery half bursting from the inside and a nail file. There's also a photo of her father and mother when they were still together. They look happy, and they must have been happy once before one of them looked for love outside the marriage. Love doesn't last. They've proved it, and now it's happened in her life too. There is no Walt Disney happy ending in real life. Someone leaves, or someone dies, and the other person is left alone to pick up the pieces.

From the photo she holds in both hands, Jasmine's blue eyes smile at her. Her blonde hair falls down her sides to her shoulders, and her teeth are white and shiny, like those of someone in a toothpaste commercial. On a scale from zero to ten, Amelia thinks she's a ten—and it's unbearable because she is not in the bedroom with her. Beauty is a monster when you can't have it for yourself.

She stares at the photo of Jasmine and places her right hand down her panties and begins masturbating. Her groin is immediately moist, and it feels as good at is hurts. It should have been Jasmine's fingers between her legs, not her own.

But then she seems to be thinking hard for a few seconds and then throws the framed photo across to the other side of the room, the glass shattering in hundred pieces. She can't do this anymore. Solo sex is not for her.

Frustrated, she stands up from the bed and walks to the wardrobe. She opens it and looks at the clothes inside it—

dresses, skirts, tank tops, jeans, blouses, tee-shirts, skimpy tops, black, yellow, red, green, blue, white, purple. There are plenty of choices, but she knows what she wants to look like for the occasion she has in mind. She goes through some of the short dresses and selects a black one that looks really small and a tight-fit—a body glove. The perfect pick-up dress, the one that's going to make her look like a slut.

Tonight, I want to be a slut.

Three minutes later she's in the bathroom applying make-up—a final touch-up of her red revival lipstick in front of the mirror. She stares at herself, and suddenly she moves forth and kisses the lips of the reflection as if she were passionately kissing another person—her eyes closed. She pulls back and smiles at herself, as if she's trying to seduce someone. The imprint of her lips are on the mirror, like a fingerprint left on a glass She pouts and then sticks her tongue out to her reflection. She is a woman now, but the heart never grows up.

When done, she leaves the bathroom and heads for the hallway.

She has trouble walking with her red high-heel shoes. They hurt her ankles, but she knows in order to look beautiful, one must suffer. It's not enough to be physically perfect from birth —you have to work hard to make it look unattainable for others. In her everyday clothes, she looks like the girl-next-door. When made up, she looks like the model she plays in front of the cameras—and some people pay outrageous money for such camouflage.

She checks herself one more time in front of the hallway entrance mirror.

Perfect.

She grabs the car keys from the mirror counter-top. She turns to the left and opens the front door, flicks the light off and steps out into the foyer.

She locks the door behind her.

16

CHAPTER THREE

The front door of the apartment is pushed open. It is quiet in the lobby, other than the sound of shoes against the concrete floor.

A shadow appears and flicks the light on.

It's Amelia.

She walks in, dressed in the same black dress she wore when she left the apartment earlier on in the night, but not looking as fresh—her hair a little more messed up, her clothes a little more worn-in. She is tired from bobbing away for a few hours. Her tight, black dress smells of alcohol, cigarettes and perspiration. Her short hair is spiked up from the sweat of working out on a dance floor like a raving lunatic.

The call of the wild.

There's a young woman with her, early twenties, a read-head with freckles, serious looking and beautiful all at once. She is shorter than Amelia, but it doesn't bother Amelia because it gives her the advantage of being *above*.

The young woman's name is Yvette—she told her so when she picked her up at a famous lesbian nightclub in Brunswick—and she is well-rounded, but not necessarily in a bad way. She has a lovely smile and large breasts. Amelia likes large breasts because hers are average, and there's something very erotically maternal about large breasts. When she sees large breasts, she just wants to touch them, put her face against them, suck on them.

The two girls say nothing and Amelia closes the front door. They are not walking straight because they are both a little intoxicated and still feel the high of a party drug so easily available at nightclubs these days.

Yvette follows Amelia and takes in her surroundings. She seems mesmerised by the 1940s look of the apartment, with its motif gold wallpaper and brown carpet. It's very New York in style, the type no longer common these days because people are too busy living to bother decorating. Amelia fell in love with the apartment when she first saw it because it looked like nothing else she had seen before.

Yvette obviously likes it too, even though she doesn't say it in words. Her wandering eyes give it away, like the eyes of a child in a chocolate shop.

Amelia turns into the bedroom from the hallway and vanishes, eager to move to the next stage. She been dancing the night away, working herself up to fucking Yvette, and now she's more than ready.

Yvette follows her to the bedroom.

Amelia pulls her black dress over her head, revealing her white, push-up bra and white, cotton panties. She pulls down her panties first, the darkness of her bush now clearly visible, glistening with pearls of sweat.

Then she removes her bra and tosses it on the floor.

Yvette pulls down her red skirt and then her black panties. She's a real red-head because her bush is also red, the colour of her hair. It's such a turn-on for Amelia. She's always had a penchant for red-heads, but she's never actually slept with one. She wonders what Yvette tastes like, and she can't wait to find out. The smell of her presence is already strong and musky, and Amelia can feel the desire not only in her groin, but all

18

over her body. She shivers from excitement even though it's warm in the bedroom because of the balmy weather outside.

Amelia climbs on the bed covered in a clean red sheet.

"Come on," she says and offers Yvette her hand.

Yvette takes it and moves onto the bed. Her back slides effortlessly against the red sheet.

They have sex—not lovemaking, just straight sex, like animals, as if they had not had sex for weeks.

Amelia sucks on Yvette's large nipples and closes her eyes. It feels too good in a way she can't really explain—maybe some infantile need to bond with the maternal body. She then pulls herself down and goes between Yvette's legs.

Yvette is moving and moaning all at once from the pleasure Amelia is giving her. She grabs on to Amelia's head and pushes her more against her vagina.

Amelia cannot control herself much longer as she fingers herself with right index and keeps on sucking inside Yvette's slit.

After Yvette comes, she pulls back from Amelia and lies to the side of the bed exhausted. She is breathing fast, the wetness between her legs now leaking onto the clean, red bed sheets.

Yvette turns her back on Amelia.

Amelia is looking at her, expecting something more. She's made Yvette come, but she hasn't come herself. She wants Yvette to go down on her too, but it looks as if it's not going to happen—not tonight anyway.

Yvette closes her eyes and goes to sleep.

Amelia moves on her back and stares at the ceiling, unable to sleep, clearly frustrated she didn't get what she had hoped for. She finishes herself off quietly, the thumb and index finger of her right hand massaging her clitoris whilst Yvette is sound asleep. She eventually comes, but it's just masturbation once more and never as satisfying as experiencing an orgasm when a girl goes down on you.

When done, she turns to the side, relieved and disappointed all at once.

It takes her another two hours before she manages to fall into a deep sleep.

Amelia wakes up from the sound of Yvette urinating in the toilet bowl, just next door to the bedroom. She reaches with her hand—Yvette's side of the bed is still warm. Her strong smell has taken over the room, and it's comforting, like a heater left on all night when the temperature outside drops to freezing point.

The light coming through the bedroom window is bright, and Amelia squints. She seems a little lost, as if she is trying to figure out where she is and who she is—a hangover from the previous night's drinking and drug taking.

When Yvette enters the bedroom again, Amelia is lying on her side, her back to the bathroom entrance. She closes her eyes and pretends to be asleep.

Yvette is totally silent as she puts on her white panties and bra. She has to make a little effort to tuck her large breasts in the bra.

Amelia can feel the weigh of her stare in her direction, but she keeps her eyes shut. She can hear Yvette breathing and smell her sex, and for a moment she wants to jump out of bed and fuck her all over again.

Yvette puts on her red skirt dress and white blouse. She is about to say something as she looks at Amelia lying vulnerably on the bed.

But she doesn't say anything.

She finishes getting dressed, looks one more time at Amelia and leaves the room.

Amelia opens her eyes and stares at an empty spot in front of her.

Then she hears the sound of the front door opening and shutting. There is disappointment written all over her face. She feels empty and dirty inside, as if she has committed an unforgivable act, which will send her soul to hell for eternity.

CHAPTER FOUR

Amelia is sitting in the corner of the white bathtub, totally naked from out-of-bed. Her dark hair is messed up, and she is still wearing the make-up from the previous night. The air from the bathroom window is cold, but she doesn't care. It awakes her senses at times when all she can feel is the pain and emptiness inside. There is a little traffic noise outside, but the rest of the world is still sound asleep. She smells the salt from the ocean half a kilometre down from the apartment coming through the open gap of the window.

With great concentration, she scratches her arm with her silver nail file—not enough to bleed, but enough to show some marks. She grimaces as she is doing this, but once done, she seems relieved, an almost-orgasmic look on her face. She has no idea why causing herself harm can feel so good, and though she has read about it on the Internet, she still doesn't fully understand it.

After she has taken this pleasurable pain to the core of her soul, she places the nail file to the side and dresses the wound on her forearm. She uses antiseptic and then covers them with flesh-coloured band-aids she had set aside for the procedure.

When done, she stands from the bathtub and walks up to the hand sink.

She looks at herself in the mirror—her solemn face indicates she hasn't slept well the previous night. She is staring at a stranger staring back at her. Her hazel eyes seems small in the mirror, almost invisible, but she knows it might be because she is still tired and should really get a few more hours sleep.

She turns the hand sink tap on and drinks from it, the water tasting like the copper pipes that carry it, and then splashes the cold water on her face. It's a strange sensation, almost as if a sheet of ice has been gently laid against her skin.

The scratches on her arm sting a little, but it helps her to not have to focus on anything else. She read somewhere how the greater pain can diminish the lesser pain, and it might just be what is happening here. Is emotional pain lesser than physical pain?

She grabs a pink towel from the rack and dries her face.

When finished, she pulls the towel from her face, looks at her face again, places the towel back on the rack and leaves the bathroom.

Amelia opens the refrigerator. The little light is dim, and she knows she needs to replace it soon, otherwise she won't be able to see what's inside the fridge at all.

She is wearing white panties and a grey tee-shirt.

There's nothing in there but half a container of skim milk. She grabs the milk, smells it to make sure it's not off, and when she decides it isn't, she drinks straight from the container.

Some of the milk runs down the side of her mouth. She wipes it with her forearm, not really caring if she catches enough or not, and then she places the container back in the door of the refrigerator.

She shuts the door.

Amelia is sitting on a park bench by herself. She is wearing fluro-pink headphones and listening to hip-hop, her head moving gently to the beat. A large shadow from a gumtree covers half her face. A dirt track leads to a children's playground with a swing made of black rubber, and a young, overweight mother in yellow tracksuit pants and her child playing in the sand pit. There's a wooden table with matching benches, a green rubbish bin and a wood-and-iron shelter opposite her. The air is cold but the sky is blue, and rain is predicted for later in the evening.

She is staring in front of her, not really caring where she is —she just had to get out of the apartment for a while because it began to feel as if her life was getting smaller and smaller. She has a sad look on her face, like someone much older, someone who has already given up on love and life—and in a way she has.

She wears a grey hoodie and a blue cap, her hands deep inside the pockets of the hoodie.

An older, attractive woman walks past her and stares, a clear come-on, daring look. She wears a floral dress in red and yellow motifs, and her brown hair is down to her shoulders. She has small eyes, feline-like in nature, and almost too severe for her appearance. It's hard to tell her age exactly, but Amelia thinks she must be in her early forties. She doesn't normally go for older women, but today she is too desperate for affection —and for sex.

Amelia locks eyes with the stranger.

The older woman holds the stare, almost amused, but a few second later she seems embarrassed. When she realises Amelia is not giving up, and this is much more than just a friendly hello, she moves on and increases her pace.

Amelia watches her walk away and keeps the stare lingering. She wonders what it would be like to hold the woman naked in bed and make love to her all night long.

The older woman doesn't look back. She walks down the end of the park, makes a sharp right and vanishes from view.

Almost at the same time Amelia's smart-phone vibrates in

her pocket. She pulls it out and reads the message on the screen: *Do you want to hook up tonight?*

She types furiously into her phone, hunched over, totally obsessed with what she is doing, as if the world around her doesn't exist.

Amelia is having sex with a total stranger—like animals. There is no passion. They are in the bedroom of her apartment, the blinds closed, but there is enough light from the outside to make-out the other lover.

The warmth and presence is what Amelia needs right now —being in proximity to another soul, feeling the sound of another heartbeat against hers.

The other woman is young, too young maybe—bottle-blond hair, red lipstick, too much foundation. She picked her up at a King Street nightclub, but many young women there are under-age and use fake identifications to get into the clubs. The other woman looked older when she picked her up, but now that she is having sex with her, Amelia believes she is about sixteen. She won't ask because of the fear the woman is not a woman but a girl. Her breasts are tiny, and her ribs almost stick out of her torso. Her arms are match-thin, and Amelia is scared she is going to break them if she tries something too adventurous.

The other woman smells of bubble gum and cheap body spray, the type you can buy at the local supermarket. She wears plastic jewellery, another indication she's much younger than she first appeared to be. She's not a very good lover and lacks experience.

Amelia guides her, directs her head between her legs and instructs her on what to do. She is clumsy and hurts Amelia as she sucks too hard on her clitoris. She has to tell her to not use her teeth so much.

When it's over, the other woman apologises for being inadequate, and she almost cries. Amelia tells her it's okay, and hugs her and lets her fall asleep against her shoulder.

She feels like a mother rather than a lover.

Amelia is asleep, her head resting on her forearms on the kitchen table. Her notebook is switched on. There's a half-filled glass of vodka and her smart-phone next to the notebook.

The smart-phone vibrates on the table-top.

It wakes her up.

She looks up at the kitchen clock: 3.10 p.m.

Outside the sky is clear blue, but the air is cold coming from the gap from the kitchen's window frame.

She checks the message on her phone. Her modelling agent has a job for her, and she needs to be there in half an hour. She replies back she will be there.

When done, she places the phone back on the table-top, and goes back to sleep for another ten minutes, her head resting on her arms.

Amelia is walking the street to get to her modelling assignment. She is dressed in a tight green top and short purple skirt. It's way too cold to be under-dressed, but she can't be bothered taking too many layers of clothes with her.

Two young men walk past her. One is taller than the other, dark-hair, somewhat overweight. They could be brothers or cousins. They look at her lustfully, and one makes a comment to the other Amelia cannot understand.

She puts her head down and ignores them.

Once she walks past them, they stare at her backside.

"Dyke," one of them yells out.

She ignores the comment and moves on.

The second man screams, "Hey! We're tal-king to you, bitch!"

She walks faster.

"Hey!" the second man continues. "Where the fuck do you

think you're going?"

She ignores them, increases her pace and turns the street corner. She enters a photography studio that appears to look like a house from the outside, her heart pounding against her ribcage like a deer that has just escaped a wolf's fangs.

Amelia is standing against a white backdrop in full make-up and pink-and-yellow flower-motif dress. She looks incredible with professional make-up applied. It took the make-up artist nearly one hour to make her look so good.

A male photographer is taking photos of her—click, click, click—a firing gun. He's tall, dark and confident.

She poses and seems to know what she is doing with relative ease. Her smile looks genuine, and she knows how to work the camera. At times she appears flirtatious and treats the camera as someone she's trying to seduce.

The photographer says, "Very good."

Bright lights and more clicking.

More posing.

More clicking.

Five minutes later she's in the studio's bathroom doing a line of coke. She doesn't do coke often because it's too expensive on her irregular salary, and she gets too dehydrated afterward. There's a reason why so many models carry bottles of water with them. It has nothing to do with them being healthy—the coke does it. It helps you to stay thin but dries your mouth like cement.

She looks up to the mirror and takes it right in. The nasal mucous membranes absorb the cocaine straight into her blood stream, and the rest is trapped by mucus, which stops it from reaching her lungs. She wipes the excess cocaine from her nose.

She stares at her face for a little while whilst the cocaine is doing its job. In no time, she feels invincible and focuses, ready to finish the job.

Then she re-touches her make-up—red lipstick and blush to hide the redness at the edges of her nostrils.

When she's done, she leaves the bathroom.

The door of the apartment opens.

It's dark.

The light is flicked on.

Amelia walks in, followed by another woman, Celia, mid-twenties. She is tall and thin, barely out of her teens. She has big, dark eyes, dark hair, but a snow-white complexion. She wears a white dress, and her red bra and underwear are visible through the dress.

She turns to Amelia. "It's your place?"

"Yes."

Like the other woman Amelia fucked the other day, Celia seems to be taken by the 1940s retro look of the apartment. She looks down the hallway and touches the patterned wallpaper with the palm of her hand.

They enter the bedroom.

Amelia removes her black dress, stocking, bra and underwear—her dark bush now exposed for her new lover to see. She seems a little drunk and nearly trips over but catches herself on the edge of the bed frame just in time.

Celia removes her white dress, red bra and matching panties. She is not as confident as Amelia, and it's obvious she's not used to having one night stands. She still has baby-fat on her body, particularly on her legs and buttocks. Her bush is untrimmed and neglected. It turns Amelia on. She is used to girls who look after themselves, and there is something animal-like in this young woman.

They have sex—not love.

Celia comes as Amelia fingers her and sucks on her nipples at the same time. Her wetness is all over Amelia's fingers, her vagina filled like a sponge.

Amelia takes her finger to her mouth—it tastes like the

white of a raw egg.

Celia pulls to the side and sits up on the bed, her cherry exposed, the lips of her vagina red and raw from being worked on.

Amelia's smart-phone vibrates. She grabs it, looks at it, and types furiously, both fingers hammering away at the same time.

Celia turns around and looks at her and says nothing. She doesn't seem happy or disap-pointed—just neutral, the way one-nigh-stand lovers do after they've had meaningless, empty sex.

She gets up and puts on her red underwear, matching bra and white dress.

Amelia is still typing like crazy.

"Who is it?" Celia asks.

She doesn't reply but keeps typing.

Celia grabs her red blouse and puts it on.

Amelia is typing.

Celia leaves the bedroom.

The sound of the front door being shut echoes in the apartment.

Suddenly, Amelia stops typing and looks around—she realises Celia has left the apart-ment. She can still smell her sex in the bedroom.

She seems a little surprised but then shrugs and continues to type on her smart-phone.

CHAPTER FIVE

Bright daylight.

A knock on the door.

Amelia opens her eyes. She's got a serious hangover, like a hammer beating her relentlessly on both sides of the head. She grabs a plastic bottle of water by the side of the bed, takes a couple of prescription pills from a vial and swallows the lot.

More knocking.

She doesn't answer but just gets up instead, almost losing her footing in the process. She puts on a pink bathrobe with a milk stain on the front and a hole at the bottom—a gift from Jasmine, and she just can't see herself getting rid of it.

More knocking, this time more insistent.

Bang! Bang! Bang!

"All right, I'm coming," she says, and then to herself: "Jesus!"

She opens the door and says nothing.

Her father, Fabien, mid-forties, walks in, looking as if he is familiar with the routine. He's almost bald and has a salt-and-pepper goatee. He is smaller than Amelia but relatively thin for his age. The glasses he wears hide the largeness of his eyes. He's neither ugly nor good looking, but somewhere in between, like someone you cross in the street and don't really notice. He wears a green polo shirt and brown pants. His shoes are black and spotless, as if he'd just bought them this morning. There is something fatherly about him, which brings Amelia comfort and discomfort all at once.

He kisses Amelia on both cheeks, the way the Europeans do. He smells of cheap, off-the-shelf cologne. "Everything okay?"

"Yes."

He looks at her as if he knows she's lying. He's about to say something, but he refrains.

"Do you want a coffee?" Amelia asks.

"I'd love one."

They walk the length of the hallway and enter the kitchen. It's relatively clean She tries to keep it neat because she never knows when he is going to drop in.

Even though she asked him if he wants coffee, she lets him make it. She can't be bothered, and he knows his way around anyway.

She sits at the kitchen table, her hands nursing her head from the hangover. This is a really bad time for him to visit, but she can't really bring herself to tell him. He would get upset, and these days he gets upset very easily. He looks calm on the surface, but he holds the frustration in and eventually it comes out like a packet of dynamite, all at once, exploding and confronting.

Fabien pours the coffee into two yellow mugs. He opens the refrigerator and grabs the only thing in there—long-life skim milk.

He says, "You should eat better."

"Yes, I know." She doesn't look at him. When he gets patronising, she doesn't want to know him. She hates to be told what to do, and how to live her life—which is why she left home in the first place, even though she can't afford it.

He unscrews the top of the milk carton and takes a sniff. It's almost insulting, but she's used to him by now.

31

"I only opened it yesterday," she says, even though she knows it would have been better to say nothing at all.

Fabien brings the yellow mugs to the table. "You seem a little strange this morning. It looks as if you've lost weight again."

Amelia stares at him for a few seconds, almost as she feels offended, but then smiles. "I worked late last night." She lies, but she doesn't care. Lying works as long as people don't know you're lying. The truth brings forth more questioning, more explanations and then more unwarranted advice.

Parents are like teachers. They cripple you with their life-long experiences, stories and advice, which have no bearing on your own existence.

Fabien places two sugar cubes in his coffee and stirs. He puts one hand on top of Amelia's. "You should come back home."

"No, I'm good here." She avoids his stare because she knows where this is going, and she cannot be bothered.

Not today.

Not this morning.

He takes a sip from his coffee. "It's lonely without you."

"Then find yourself another woman."

"Yes, well, you know—it's not exactly my fault."

"I know, you've told me a hundred times before."

Fabien is about to reply, but she prolongs avoiding eye contact, so he doesn't bother further. She knows he knows she's in one of those moods, and pushing his luck means she's probably going to say something wrong, and then they'll argue, and they'll both end up regretting it.

Amelia stares at her untouched coffee, but she doesn't want any. Coffee and migraines do not go well together.

Finally, after a few seconds of awkward silence, she says, "I need to get some air."

She pushes her chair back, stands up, and leaves her coffee cup untouched.

Fabien says, "I'm coming with you."

"If you want."

He begins to follow her.

She says, "Hey, you are going to let me have a shower and get dressed first? Yes?"

Fabien stops and steps back. "Oh, yes, sure—sorry."

She leaves the kitchen.

He sits back at the kitchen table and drinks his coffee, sadness etched on his face like charcoal on paper.

Amelia and Fabien are walking side-by-side down the street, past the other apartments from her neighbourhood. The traffic is relatively congested and the air smells of exhaust fumes. She wears a pair of grey tracksuit pants and a red tee-shirt, not bothering to look pretty. It's always the same after a night of partying and sex—the morning after, all your energy is spent on trying to keep your head clear for longer than a minute.

They don't say anything, like two strangers walking side-by-side by accident.

An older man, jeans and casual yellow shirt, is closing in on them from behind.

Amelia turns around and then turns to Fabien. "I think I've been followed."

The man walks past them.

"No, you're not," Fabien says. "You're getting a little paranoid lately."

She says nothing. He's probably right. It's the prescription and the non-prescription drugs that make her paranoid.

And the lack of sleep.

And the lack of love.

They walk on to the front of a cafe with unpainted brick walls, high windows with white frames, and stencilled writing on the glass door. It looks very continental even though they are halfway around the world. The immigrants brought in a wealth of cake-making and gastronomic ingenuity when they arrived decades ago with nothing but suitcases and dreams of a better life.

Amelia and Fabien stop, look at the windows for a few seconds. There is an assortment of pastries—muffins, bagels, eclairs, croissants.

Fabien says, "Let's go in, they do lunch here too—my treat."

He leads, and she follows to the entrance.

They go inside.

Fabien's plate is virtually empty, but he is still eating. There is now only a hint of a salad and focaccia on his plate, and his glass of orange juice is only one quarter full.

Amelia's plate is nearly full—Agrigento salad with a toast on the side. She is texting on her smart-phone instead of eating.

It's quiet in the cafe, and they are the only two people sitting at the table having lunch. The smell of freshly-brewed coffee lingers in the air like warm sunlight on a spring day.

Fabien says, "Who is it?"

Amelia doesn't reply and keeps typing.

Fabien seems a little embarrassed to be sitting there with her playing with her phone, even though the only other person in the room is the cafe owner, a man in his early thirties with blond tips and a manicured beard. "Is it important?"

She doesn't look up. "No, it's just Facebook."

"Ah!" He says as if he knows what she's talking about—but he hasn't a clue because he's not up with social networking and the speed at which the Internet has turned the world upside-down.

She finishes typing and looks up. "What were you saying?"

He looks at her, then at her untouched salad and toast, then back at her. "You haven't eaten your food."

She rolls her eyes and forces herself to eat what's on the

plate.

Amelia is in the toilet cubicle of the cafe.

She sticks two fingers inside her mouth and forces herself to vomit. She throws up the food she's just eaten—lettuce, pasta, tomatoes, roasted peppers, artichokes, mushrooms, olives and toast, all washed with grapefruit juice.

She flushes and wipes the seat with toilet paper.

When she's done, she makes her way to the hand sink. She cleans herself up with a paper towel and water from the tap.

She looks at herself in the mirror and applies her lipstick one tone darker than her natural colour.

With her index finger, she removes a food speck—mushroom—from the corner of her bottom lip. She wipes the speck on the paper towel.

She arranges her hair in the mirror, looks satisfied and leaves the bathroom.

Amelia is playing tennis against the wall at the Peanut Farm Reserve in St Kilda. The sky is blue and cloudless. The air warm like maple syrup. She wears her usual yellow top, blue shorts and white tennis shoes.

Fabien is watching her.

She hits the ball back every single time, and to anyone's eyes, she would seem to be quite accomplished.

Five minutes later, when she's done, she packs her red tennis racket and three yellow tennis balls in a pink zip-up bag standing near the side of the brick wall.

She takes off, and Fabien walks next to her.

She is sweaty and exhausted and just wants to go home to a hot shower.

Fabien says, "You play well."

"Not really," Amelia says.

"Have you lost more weight?"

"Oh, you're getting really annoying—you're going to tell me

I've lost weight every time you see me?"

She storms off in front of him.

Fabien seems defeated. He waits a few seconds and then goes after her. "Wait a sec!"

When they arrive at her apartment fifteen minutes later, they stand by the front door of the building.

"Where's Jasmine?" Fabien says.

"On holidays," Amelia says.

"When will she be back?"

"I don't know—whenever she feels like it."

Fabien thinks this over. "You're still a couple?"

"Yes, of course." She kisses him on the cheek. "I have to go." She doesn't wait for a reply and quickly enters the apartment foyer.

He watches her enter the apartment, a concerned look on his face.

She closes the door on him before he has time to say a word.

He watches her climb the stairs through the door glass panel. He is like a lost puppy, which is never going to find its way home.

CHAPTER SIX

Amelia is sitting naked on the toilet of her apartment, urinating, the door wide open. The traffic outside hums like bubble bees.

Her smart-phone buzzes.

A message.

She reads it:

Are you free tonight?

She types back a message.

My place. Don't be late.

There's a small party happening at Amelia's apartment.

There are only girls there, and the music is techno and loud enough for the neighbours to hear it across the street. Amelia likes playing music loud when she has friends around, but no one ever complains—not upstairs, not downstairs, not even from the across the street.

Amelia seems overly happy, almost as if she's faking it. She wears a tight, mid-riff, white top that shows her nipples and exposes her belly button, and a pair of stone-washed jeans she picked up at the Mission Store on Chapel Street where she drops in once a week to check new items. Her hair is gelled up in spikes, and she rinsed it with a rust colour, which makes her look like a character from one of the early *Mad Max* films.

It is somewhat of a relief how she can put her mind on something else than Jasmine. The music is pumping in her blood, in her heart, in her brain. She loves dancing, and when she was with Jasmine, they used to go clubbing every weekend in the city and on Chapel Street. They got thrown out once before they were drunk and were making out on the dance floor, and not just kissing, but indulging in a frottage session in front of the crowd. The men at the club loved it and cheered them on—Amelia and her lover were quite aware how one of the most fetishist sexual fantasy for males is girl-on-girl, and they purposely teased them with their act—but the manager didn't want to get fined for allowing intoxicated patrons at his club, or at the worst having his club shut down.

The girls at the party are talking to one another, mouth-to-ear, like people gossiping at the office, but the music is so loud, they can't really hear anything—it's a big flirting session, where girls assess one another to establish who they are going to spend the rest of the night with. Some come for the company, some come for the sex, some come because they have nothing else to do.

Amelia dances with another girl, Stéphanie, same age—they seem to know each other quite well. Stéphanie also has short hair and wears a tight, black dress. But she's not gay, and it doesn't bother either of them. They have known each other since high school, and this has made the friendship stronger then it would have normally. School experiences have a way of binding souls like genetics bind races.

They dance as if they are possessed.

They dance provocatively, rubbing shoulders, faces so close to one another, it would appear to an outsider they are about to be mating. There is something sexually-charged between the two of them, and they seem to know it and enjoy it.

The other girls cheer them on and eventually join them.

When they are done Amelia moves to the kitchen,

exhausted from the dancing, but worked up enough for anything else that might come. She's feeling extremely horny and it's only a matter of time before she's seriously going to hit on one of the girls.

Amelia opens the refrigerator and removes a one-litre bottle of Vodka tucked alongside the chocolate swirl ice-cream from the freezer compartment.

There are some of the party-goers around her, girls who have now moved on to the what-do-you-do stage of the flirting.

She pours herself a large glass.

From her pocket, she removes a vial and takes a couple of pills. She places them in her mouth and swallows them with the Vodka. Alcohol and prescription pills don't mix, but the only people who tell you so are those who haven't tried.

A woman, twenty-something, walks up to her. "Hi, I'm Michelle."

Amelia turns around and checks Michelle out from head-to-toe. She has short, bottle-blond hair, and she is shaped more like a boy than a girl. But her eyes are kind and the same blue as a swimming pool. There is something innocently attractive about her, even though Amelia knows there is no one innocent in the world where she lives.

Amelia smiles and then, without warning, French-kisses Michelle.

Michelle and Amelia are having sex.

Amelia is really high on alcohol and prescription pills.

Michelle comes. "Fuck, yeah!"

She pulls her head back as Amelia performs cunnilingus on her—no two girls taste the same.

When done, Amelia pulls back from between Michelle's legs and sits to the side of the bed, looking as if she doesn't care at all one way or the other.

Amelia wakes up, the light from the bedroom window hitting her like a hammer.

She turns around, but Michelle is gone—the red sheets and white pillow messy on Michelle's side of the bed. The room smells of sex and alcohol.

Amelia stumbles out of bed, her whitetee-shirt and stone-washed jeans from the night before all over the floor. She holds her hand to her face for a few seconds, as if she is going to pass out.

She nearly falls over.

Shit!

She manages to catch herself on the side of the wooden bed frame.

She walks to the kitchen.

The kitchen is a mess of food, half-filled glasses and trash everywhere—beer bottles, chips, peanuts, sandwiches. There is no one left in the apartment.

Amelia opens the freezer, grabs the bottle of Vodka from the previous night, unscrews the cap and takes a swing. She catches the heat from the alcohol right down the back of throat, then down her oesophagus and her stomach.

She places the bottle on the kitchen table, walks to the window overlooking the street below and lets the alcohol sink in. It's as if someone just punched her in the face.

A few seconds later, she throws up in the kitchen sink.

Amelia is having a shower, her head under the steaming hot water. She is in a half-trance of alcohol, drugs and lack of sleep. The heat from the water feels good. She wishes she could stay here forever and never have to worry about money, work, girls, sex, food, belonging, rent, loneliness, love, jealousy, fear.

Amelia is sitting at a desk facing Dr Keener.

He's a bony man, mid-fifties, who wears tortoise shell

glasses, a white business shirt and black slacks. His brown eyes are almost colourless, as if the passing of time has drained the pigmentation out of them. His brown hair is receding, showing a larger-than-average, wrin-kle-free forehead. He seems at ease with himself, and it makes her feel somewhat uncom-fortable. She doesn't understand how older people completely manage to accept who they are, irrespective of what others might think. She wishes she could be the same, but she also knows growing older also means getting closer to death. As much as life can be an unbearable burden at times, she's not ready to die just yet.

The office is bare of any form of decoration. Everything is brown and grey and monotone. It's very masculine and clinical all at once, maybe purposely designed to not invoke any particular feelings on the patients. It smells of furniture polish and a musky, male aftershave.

Amelia is waiting as the psychiatrist writes something on his yellow prescription pad.

"You're taking too many tablets," he says matter-of-factly without looking up.

"If you don't give me what I want, I'll get it somewhere else," Amelia says.

Dr Keener looks at her for a few seconds and shakes his head. He finishes writing the prescription.

He hands over the prescription and smiles an awkward smile. "I'll see you next Wednesday then."

Amelia notices him glancing at her breasts for a split-second, and a knot forms in her stomach. She chooses to say nothing, even though it had happened in the past. He is a man, after all, she tells herself and forgives his perverted mind.

She takes the prescription, stands up and leaves the room without saying goodbye.

Amelia is typing in her notebook. She is seated at a wooden writer's desk in the lounge room, next to a balcony overlooking the street below. The traffic is loud enough to be heard, but not loud enough to bother her. The temperature is in the mid-twenties, pleasant enough to let fresh air flow throughout the apartment.

There's a bottle of Vodka next to her and a glass half-full. There are also some prescription pills she got from the pharmacy.

Her smart-phone is on the table next to her.

She is focused. Her eyes wonder from one side of the screen to the other—she has 452 Facebook friends, and yet she is alone in her apartment. The irony hits her hard.

The smart-phone vibrates.

She looks at it, reads and then puts it down.

She continues to type on the computer.

The phone rings this time.

She looks at it, hesitates for a few seconds and finally picks it up. "Yes?"

It's her agent who says she's got a job for her and needs her to turn up as soon as possible.

"Now?" Amelia asks.

"Yes, now. Someone dropped out at the last second, and they can't re-schedule the shoot.'

"Okay."

Amelia cuts off the connection and puts the phone on the table top.

She logs off Facebook and closes the cover of her notebook.

Amelia is posing in a sexy outfit—a Bronte dress, Kiara necklace, Chrysler belt, a Jet Set bangle and Safari Wedges.

She is with a male model—early thirties, chiselled jaw, well-defined broad shoulders, firm pecs and biceps, honed hips, washboard stomach, short hair. He wears Emporio Armani designer jeans and a white Gucci shirt.

They pretend to be really taken with one another.

He removes her shirt.

The male photographer clicks away. He is mid-thirties and very tall. He's very good at his job, and the camera acts as an extension of his hand and eyes.

"Good, very good," he says.

More clicking.

More posing.

Flashes.

Amelia puts on a happy face. She is very good at pretending. She looks healthy, happy an in control of her life.

The photographer stops shooting. "Okay, we're done here."

Amelia now looks depressed and unhappy.

She goes to her yellow, plastic handbag and retrieves her smart-phone and check for messages. She types furiously and with great concentration.

The phone beeps back at her.

There's a text message.

Screw you, bitch!

She seems a little concerned and puts the phone back in her bag.

Amelia is seated by herself in a heritage tram build in the 1950s and restored to perfection in green and cream. She looks out the window at the people in the street—everyone is rushing to some unknown destination. It's a warm day and the sky is blue. The air smells of jasmine and fruits.

Her expression is pensive, in a dream-like state, as if she knows she's missing out on something—as if she's the only one who doesn't know what's going on and is unsure about what life is all about. *Or is it the same for everyone, and we all pretend to know what's going on?*

She opens her yellow, plastic bag and pops in a couple of prescription pills from an orange vial and swallows them without water.

Amelia walks out of a newsagency, a magazine in her hand. She opens the magazine and flicks through the pages.

There are photos of her modelling form the session she did with the male model the other day.

She looks happy, as if she's got the world at her feet. The cheque from her agent hasn't come through yet, but she has assured Amelia it would be sent any day now.

Amelia is typing on her notebook. She is seated at the kitchen table, looking through the window at the an elm tree that half conceals the neighbour's 1960s brick building. She is wearing white panties and grey tee-shirt. Her hair is a little messy, but she's had a shower only half an hour earlier to wake her up from her slumber of pills and alcohol. Boiling showers normally do the work, like entering a trance when you are under them, but somehow miraculously refreshing after you turn the taps off.

There's a knock on the front door of the apartment. She is not expecting anyone.

Who could this be at this time of the day?

She gets up and leaves the kitchen, the lid of the laptop open.

Slowly, she walks down the length of the hallway and thinks maybe it's a neighbour who needs her help for something.

Or maybe it's a package being delivered from an Ebay purchase, but she doesn't remember what it might be right at this minute.

When she opens the front door, she is somewhat surprised to see Yvette. Her lover is wearing a black dress and white top and smells of strawberry shampoo and cheap perfume. Her red hair is more vibrant and amber in the daylight. Her skin is winter white. Her Celtic genetics are painted all over her features—her ancestors were strong women, many who were once warriors and leaders of warfare. That character attribute is still present in today's women of Celtic ancestry, and it somehow turns Amelia on as she feels a noticeable sensation in her groin area.

"Come in," Amelia says. "I was just working in the kitchen." Working in this case means running through the news feeds of her digital friends on Facebook, most of which she has never met in real life.

Yvette smiles and enters the apartment. Even though she's been there before, she still looks around as if it were the first time. Nothing has changed since she'd been there last, except it's the first time she sees the apartment during the day. The retro gold-and-brown wallpaper seems a lighter tone in the daylight, which travels from the bedroom and bathes the hallway with the warmth of the sun.

Amelia walks back to the kitchen with Yvette right behind her.

The smell of coffee is strong from a fresh pot Amelia made earlier on that morning.

Amelia bends over the kitchen table top, logs off Facebook and closes her notebook.

Yvette walks up to her. She places one hand on Amelia's right hip and squeezes gently.

Amelia's smart-phone on the table buzzes.

She picks it up.

Yvette snatches the phone from Amelia with her left hand and places it back on the kitchen table.

"Not now," Yvette says.

Amelia doesn't protest. She likes to be dominant in a relationship, but a change is good. Maybe with Yvette they can reverse the roles and introduce some novelty in the predictable games of sex she is accustomed to.

Amelia turns around and faces her lover.

Yvette wraps her arms around her waist.

Her face is so close, Amelia can see all the details—freckles, clean skin, blue eyes, long eyelashes, red lips.

They French-kiss and move to the bedroom.

Yvette peels off her clothes and sits on the bed, her legs slightly spread apart. Amelia is still taken by her red bush and large breasts. She finds them comfortable and erotic all at once.

The room smells of night sleep and the shades are half-way down.

Amelia walks up to the side table and inserts an Annette Hanshaw compact disc into a small, black boom box and presses the play button.

The jazz-influenced pop music pours from the speaker and fills the room.

Amelia dances in front of Yvette—a slow, sexy dance to seduce Yvette.

Yvette smiles and seems surprised, but enchanted all at once.

Amelia moves her body smoothly, arms outstretched, hips swinging to the rhythm of the song. Slowly she moves closer and closer to Yvette, who is quite taken by the performance.

Amelia goes down on her knees and moves her face closer to Yvette's red bush, all the while looking up at her and making eye contact.

Then she goes down on Yvette and gently licks the outer lip of her vagina.

Yvette moves back on the bed, and with her left hand pushes Amelia's head further against her pussy.

The taste of Yvette's is strong, like some exotic foreign spice. Her tongue moves back-and-forth like a gentle summer wave.

Yvette is grunting in pleasure and eventually climaxes.

Yvette is asleep, her flamed hair unkempt, like someone who's been on a long journey and is now at peace—a warrior princess resting from battle.

Amelia watches her like a parent looks at her child. She can still feel the taste of her sex in her mouth and wants some more. But she doesn't want to wake up Yvette.

Little princess needs her beauty sleep.

Amelia leaves Yvette alone in the bedroom and walks quietly to the bathroom.

She removes a silver nail file from the white cabinet attached to the wall above the sink, sits on the tiled floor, her back against the hardness of the bathtub, and draws scratches on her left forearm.

She is focused.

The pain is good.

When she draws blood, she almost reaches orgasm. She licks the blood from the wound and sucks some of it in. The coppery taste gives her temporary relief from the raging confusion in her brain.

When done, she places the nail file down on the hand sink, not worried about washing it.

She longs for Yvette to ejaculate in her mouth again.

Amelia wakes up.

The sunlight through the bedroom window is blinding, like a fist in the face.

She has a serious hangover. The cut on her upper arm burns. Maybe she cut too deep last night. It happens sometimes when she's not totally lucid, particularly after drinking and taking prescription tablets. She'll need to sooth the burn with antiseptic, and also clean the cut to avoid getting it infected.

She turns around, but Yvette is not on her side of the bed. The smell of her lover lingers even after she's gone, and Amelia moves to where Yvette has slept and inhales the reminder of her presence. She can still taste Yvette at the back of her throat and wishes she was here in her arms. Waking up alone is one of the most depressing facts about being single. She knows she'll never get used to it.

Slowly, she stumbles out of bed—the floor hard and

uninviting—and puts on her pink robe.

She leaves the bedroom and enters the kitchen. The blinds are down, and the room is bathed in semi-darkness. It smells of vodka from the previous night and coffee left in a pot twenty-four hours ago.

She notices a hand-written note next to her notebook. She grabs the white piece of paper torn from a page of her small, red buffalo journal.

It reads: *I can't do this anymore. You have to stop doing this shit.*

She crumples the paper and throws it on the floor. She crosses the length of the kitchen, opens the refrigerator, grabs a carton of skim milk and drinks straight from it. It's cold and helps her to wake up from her slumber.

She is a lost soul now, desperate to find her way home.

She lets the carton of milk fall to the floor and leaves the fridge door open. She doesn't care to pick it up or clean the mess left behind. She goes back to the bedroom to catch up on some sleep.

Amelia is walking St Kilda beach by herself.

The air is warm and smells salty and the sky a cloudless blue. There's traffic on the Esplanade, but the buzzing of the engines is distant, almost as if it were her imagination.

She notices a heterosexual couple on a wooden bench, kissing and hugging—they are young and beautiful, particularly the girl. She wears a yellow tank top and a denim mini-skirt. She has blonde hair and a cute button nose. Amelia can see the pink of her panties from the distance. She wants her but she knows she can't have her. The problem with sex is the more you have it, the more you want it.

She stares at the couple for a little too long, and they notice and stare back at her.

She walks on to where the pier begins and aims for the Little Blue restaurant at the end of the pier.

Amelia is getting make-up put on by a professional make-up artist—male, bald, mid-thirties—at a photo-shoot studio. The room is small with lights around the mirrors and curtains for privacy.

The make-up artist transforms her from a sick-looking young woman to a world-class model.

When the make-up artist is done, he leaves.

Amelia stares at her reflection and wonders who is this person staring back at her. She looks happy, but she knows she is not. She wonders how many people look happy on the surface when they are really suffering on the inside.

She moves on to the photo-shoot in the room next door.

It's a large white-washed room with lights and reflectors.

Various poses with ease—she looks sexy and seductive. She flirts with the camera like someone flirts with a prospective lover.

Click, click, click.

Back at the kitchen of her apartment, Amelia is checking her Facebook news feed.

Suddenly, there is a knock on the door.

She leaves the kitchen and walks down the length of the hallway.

When she opens the door, a tall, dark man is standing in front of her. They met at a nightclub last year and exchanged phone numbers.

He's now her regular drug supplier.

They don't say anything, but just exchange coke for money, like they have done hundreds of times before.

She closes the door and returns to the kitchen. The coke comes in a little bag, and she can't wait to have a line.

She opens the bag and does a line straight on the kitchen table. The coke hits her brain almost immediately, and she feels like a million dollars. She knows it's going to make it impossible for her to go to sleep, but she doesn't care.

She tried the so-called legal alternative to coke, a synthetic mix of whatever is available at the time, but it's never the same as coke.

Coke is expensive, and given the little money she has, she knows she can't really afford it.

But she can't also afford to go through the day without some kind of stimulant, otherwise she's going to end up cutting herself to the point of no-return.

Amelia is sitting up on the bed reading O*n The Road*.

She stops reading and looks at the photo of Jasmine. Her blue eyes look back at her, the way they use to in real life. Her former lover has a perfect skin, perfect teeth and perfect blond hair. She couldn't believe it when Jasmine agreed she would go out with her. She felt Jasmine was way above her standard.

And now Jasmine is gone, Amelia thinks how maybe Jasmine only used her because she had no one else at the time.

Amelia sniffles once, twice. She thinks maybe she caught a cold, and this is the beginning of an out-of-season flu. She wipes the her nostril with her hand and looks at the blood.

Shit!

She runs to the bathroom, the blood coming out twice as strong as when it first began.

A burst blood vessel.

She stands in front of the mirror. She tries to stop the bleeding with cotton balls whilst lifting her head back. It takes nearly a minute for the blood to stop.

When done, she steps in the shower.

The water is running cold.

She is still high from the coke, and her body is revved up like a car engine on maximum rpm.

Amelia is sitting at a bus stop, reading her Kerouac novel.

A young woman, Goth, sits next to her. She has too much make-up on and looks sad.

Amelia turns and looks at her.

The young woman stares back.

They lock eyes for a few seconds—intense and charged.

They know.

Back at the apartment, Goth and Amelia are in bed. They just finished having sex.

Amelia's smart-phone vibrates.

She picks it up and looks at the screen.

She turns to Goth. "You have to go."

Goth shrugs, gets up from the bed and dresses.

Amelia puts on her robe.

She takes the young woman to the front door of the apartment and lets her out.

Amelia smiles and closes the door behind her.

Fabien and Amelia are having coffee in the kitchen. He wears a five-dollar red buttoned-up shirt and a pair of ten-dollar jeans. She is still in white panties and grey tee-shirt, freshly out of bed in the middle of the day.

Outside the sky is blue and the air is warm. The door of the balcony is wide-open, and the sound of the traffic below circulates through the apartment.

Fabien says, "Who's the young woman I saw in the hallway?"

"Who?"

"Average height, dark hair, a lot of make-up, dressed in black, gold jewellery."

Amelia hesitates for a few seconds. She looks down at her coffee. "Oh, a neighbour."

"Ah!" He pauses for a few seconds. "But it looks as if she's come out of your apartment?"

"Nope."

It's obvious he doesn't believe her, but he is not pressing further.

They drink their coffee in silence.

Amelia's smart-phone vibrates on the table top.

She picks it up and reads.

She types with both her thumbs.

Fabien says, "You sleep with this thing?"

Amelia is not listening. She continues to type.

Fabien swallows the rest of his coffee and stands up. "I have to go to the bathroom."

Amelia doesn't look up. "Okay."

He leaves the kitchen and tries to catch her eye to no avail.

She's still typing.

He gives up and leaves the room

Amelia stares at her phone.

In the bathroom, Fabien washes his hands in the hand sink. He notices a bit of blood around the rim of the plug hole.

Amelia walks in on him. "Everything all right?"

He looks at her, clearly worried. He looks as if he is going to say something important, but instead he says, "Yes."

He walks to her and hugs her awkwardly.

She doesn't really return the hugging but just lets him do it. She's almost pulling back—afraid of being loved.

"I'll see you soon," Fabien says.

He kisses her on the cheek and leaves the bathroom.

Amelia waits, almost as if she thinks he's going to come back.

She hears the front door opening and shutting.

She stands in silence.

After a few seconds, she sits on the edge of the bathtub and cries non-stop for ten minutes.

On the Thursday of the same week in a deserted country town, somewhere on the Bellarine Coast, only ten minutes drive from the ocean, Amelia is walking alone by herself. She can't shake off a terrible and engulfing fear of loneliness. She misses Jasmine terribly, and she almost wishes she had never met her. This way she wouldn't have to deal with a broken heart.

The sun is high in the blue sky, but the air is cold, and with only a thin, green wool jumper to cover her skin, she realises if she doesn't get back home soon, she's going to catch a cold.

Amelia is eating by herself in an outdoor cafe. Other people are in pairs or in threes, and they seem to be happy.

A couple and a little terrier dog walk past the cafe. They smile at each other, and it makes Amelia sick to her stomach. She can't stand others being so in love with one another anymore. It's a constant reminder of what she used to have and what she no longer has.

After two cups of coffee, she leaves the cafe and walks up to the beach, only ten minutes away.

When she reaches the ocean, she sits on the sand, her back against the stone wall, which stops high-tide seawater from streaming into the road, where the traffic seems to be humming night and day, seven days a week.

The salty smell and the vastness of the ocean bring her some comfort in acknowledging we are nothing in this world —just creatures in transit from one plane to another.

Or maybe from nothingness to oblivion.

Amelia is standing in front of the open wardrobe of her room. Three quarters of the wardrobe is filled with her clothes. One third are Jasmine's clothes, and there's an obvious gap between the two sets of clothing. Jasmine left in a rush and never took her clothes with her. She said she would be back to pick them up, but she hasn't bothered yet, and Amelia had to bring them to the new apartment.

Amelia grabs one of Jasmine's yellow shirts and brings it to her face.

She takes a deep breath from the shirt. It's smells like

Jasmine, so much so, it's as if she standing right there next to her.

She slides her left hand down her panties and begins to masturbate while inhaling the odour of Jasmine from the shirt.

When she's done, she wipes herself with Jasmine's shirt.

Amelia is having a photo-shoot session. She wears a white bodysuit, a gold bracelet and matching necklaces.

She is halfway through it, and then she loses her composure and nearly trips over.

The photographer looks at her for a few seconds. "Wait a moment," he says and leaves the room.

Amelia is left by herself, a little dazzled.

She grabs the bag she left to the side of the room, opens it and grabs a vial of pills and a small, plastic bottle of water. She washes the pills down with the water.

Dizzy now, she sits to the side, her back against the wall. Her knees up, she rests her head on her arms.

The photographer walks back into the room. He seems a little edgy, just the way he walks and the drained look on his face.

"We're done for today," he says firmly, like a parent who tells a child to go to the corner after she's been caught doing something naughty.

Amelia tries to make eye contact with him, but he just walks out of the room.

She is left by herself, somewhat confused. She doesn't know what she's done, but she realises how from this moment her life is about to take a turn for the worse.

Again.

Amelia is sitting at the kitchen table. Her notebook is switched on. Her smart-phone is on the table-top. She feels heat on her face, not because it's not in the room but because she hates putting herself in a situation where survival depends on others.

She picks up the phone and dials. She waits for the ringing down and for someone to pick-up on the other end.

"Hello?" the voice says.

"Hello, it's Amelia...I..."

"Oh, it's you. Well, I'm sorry but we won't be able to use you anymore. You're just wasting our time, and as you know time is money."

"I know, but, I... just wasn't feeling well this morning."

"It's not the first time it has happened. I don't know what is going on with you, but you can't even stand straight for a minute. Are you on drugs or something? You do know we don't allow drugs in the workplace. This is not negotiable, and we cannot run the risk of working with models who use drugs."

Amelia is a little taken back. Her modelling agent has never spoken to her harshly in the past. She sounds really angry, and her tone is almost a scream.

"Okay, I understand but I swear it will never happen again..."

"I'm sorry, but we're going to have to let you go."

"I am begging you...without my job, I won't have any money."

"I'm sorry. I'm sure another agency would be happy to take your on. You're still marketable—but if you keep on taking drugs, you won't be for much longer."

Amelia is about to reply, but suddenly the line is dead. She pulls the phone away from her ear and looks at it as if it has a life of its own.

After a few seconds, she throws the phone across the room, and the cover goes flying one way, and the battery another way.

In the bathroom, Amelia scratches herself on the inside of her leg with the nail file.

She is focused.

When done, she cleans the wounds with antiseptic and cotton balls. She applies two band-aids across the wounds.

She looks relieved, as if all the energy has been sapped out of her.

CHAPTER SEVEN

Amelia and Fabien are sitting on a park bench.

She is staring in front of her, not really wanting to be here with her father. The air is warm enough to be outside, but not warm enough to walk around in a shirt only.

Fabien is trying to make eye contact, and she can sense it, but she is here for a specific reason and not because of his companionship. She doesn't know if other girls' fathers are as annoying as he can be, always giving her advice and telling her how she should live her life.

He never bothers her about her sexuality—not after she got angry at him and accused him of homophobia.

"You can come back home, you know," he says, his voice weak, almost as if he is begging. She hates it when he puts on this helpless tone, as if he were the victim, and she was the abuser.

She says, "No, Jasmine will be back soon."

She can see from the corner of her eye he is tired and disappointed. He probably thought she'd be married by now, and maybe even have a child.

He takes her hand in his.

She lets him, like a doll, not resisting but not reacting back either.

He says, "You know, maybe she's never coming back—you need to believe it's a possibility."

"She'll be back."

"Mum never came back."

"It's not the same."

"Ah, you're right there—it wasn't my fault."

"You're going to blame her forever?"

She pulls back her hand.

Awkward silence, then she turns to him and makes eye contact. "Can you lend me some money?" she asks, her voice is not as strong as hoped it would be.

"Ah! Is something wrong?"

"I haven't got much work at the moment—I don't even have enough to pay the rent."

"Yes, of course. You know, modelling is not exactly a stable job. You should go back to study—you got into law after all."

She can feel herself blushing. "Are you going to lend me the money or not? I didn't come here to listen to one of your sermons."

Fabien is a little shocked. She very rarely gets angry at him. "Ah, no, I mean yes," he says, "I will lend you the money, I was just saying that perhaps..."

Amelia stands from the bench. "You're annoying, you know. It's your fault mum left us."

She walks away.

"Amelia!" he shouts after her.

She turns her head whilst walking away. "Get lost!"

She walks off and leaves him alone on his bench like a miserable sod.

There's a knock on the door of the apartment.

Amelia leaves the kitchen, walks down the hallway and opens the door.

It's her drug dealer.

58

He hands over a little white bag filled with cocaine.

Amelia says, "Can I pay you later?"

The drug dealer is surprised. "I'm sorry, but no can do." He snatches the bag of cocaine back from her.

"Please, just this time!"

"Sorry"

He takes off.

Amelia sticks her head outside of the apartment and into the foyer. "Please!"

He doesn't reply, and she hears his footsteps reaching the ground-floor of the apartment.

She waits a few seconds and shuts the door.

She walks away from the door and goes back to the kitchen.

In the bedroom, Amelia is sitting against the wall opposite the queen-size bed. She feels hot and cold all at once, her stomach knotting itself like a rope.

No cocaine left.

No money.

She cries and has a mini-fit.

Amelia is sitting on a bench in the park opposite her apartment next to an older woman who is talking on her cell phone.

The sky is cloudy and grey, but it's a pleasant day to be outdoors. There's traffic noise in the distance and birds chirping.

The woman is well-dressed—a black jacket, white blouse and black pants. She could be on her lunch break from work.

Amelia is dressed casually, sunglasses and a hoodie. It's impossible to tell if she's a boy or a girl. She wears grey, cotton pants and black training shoes. There's a large, bone-coloured carry bag hanging from her right shoulder.

Next to the woman is her brown, leather handbag.

The woman notices Amelia and turns around a little in

order to have some privacy with her conversation.

Amelia looks down to where the handbag is. It's unzipped, and there is a black purse clearly visible.

The woman is busy chatting on the phone. It sounds like a private conversation, but Amelia only catches a word here and there, and she's not really interested in what the woman is saying.

Amelia looks around her to see if anyone notices anything. They are the only two people in the park, and the park is secluded enough and no one can see them from the surrounding apartments.

When Amelia thinks it's safe, she discreetly puts one hand in the handbag and takes the purse. She places the purse in her own bag.

Amelia stands and walks away from the bench.

She walks around the corner and stops in front of a rubbish bin. She removes the purse she's stolen and goes through the contents. She tosses a few items in the rubbish bin—driver's license, loyalty cards, business cards, gym membership. She pulls out two one-hundred-dollar notes and one fifty-dollar note and puts them in her bag. She also keeps a Mastercard and a Visa card.

She finds a little paper folded in one of the purses pockets. On it are little four digit numbers—the personal identification numbers from the cards. Not exactly what banks recommend to their customers.

Too easy.

She folds the paper and puts in her pocket.

Ten minutes later, Amelia is withdrawing money from an automatic teller machine. She reads the numbers on the piece of paper she stole from the woman.

The money comes out of the machine. She pockets the money and walks off quickly.

Later in the evening, back at the apartment, she is eating pasta and sauce she's made from a can and a packet. It doesn't taste good, but she's hungry and knows she needs to eat something, otherwise she's going to feel too exhausted.

There's a knock on the front door of the apartment.

Amelia walks to the door.

She opens the door.

Her drug dealer is standing in front of her. He hands over a little white bag filled with cocaine.

She hands him a bunch of notes she got from the automatic teller machine.

He takes it and says, "Nice to be doing business with you."

She doesn't reply. She is still angry at him for not giving her the drug the other day and let her pay later. He knows she was good for it.

He walks off.

She closes the door and goes back down the hallway.

In the bedroom Amelia is doing cocaine on her bed. Her legs are crossed and her head down. She takes it in. She falls back on the sheets and enjoys the trip.

The world is mine, and I can do whatever I want.

The sunlight hits Amelia in the eye. It's mor-ning, and she forgot to pull down the blinds the night before.

She turns around slowly, groans, and tries to wake up from her slumber. It's painful, and she seems to be feeling it in the depth of her bones.

She falls out of bed.

She picks herself up, a bruise on her forehead and struggles to the bathroom.

She hasn't slept all night because of the coke, and now she feels tired beyond belief. But she doesn't want to spend the whole day in bed.

Under the hot shower, she almost falls asleep and holds onto the glass panel for support.

61

And then she remembers she has an appoint-ment with her doctor.

CHAPTER EIGHT

Amelia is sitting opposite Dr Keener.

He is looking at a file on her.

He then looks at her.

She looks at him.

Silence.

He finally says, "Are we going to spend the whole day staring at one another, or are you going to share something with me?"

She just stares at him, anger written all over her face. Right now, if she had a gun, she would shoot him in the face.

He writes something in his notes.

He says, "The less you say, the longer this is going to take."

She stares at him a little longer.

"What do you want to know?" she says.

"You can begin by telling me about those scratches on your arms."

The bastard has seen the cuts.

Amelia plays with the sleeve ending of her mauve jumper. "Okay, but this is going to sound worse than it really is..."

"Tell me."

She hesitates. "I..."

Dr Keener stares at her, clearly expecting some kind of explanation.

"I don't need to tell you—it's totally irre-levant," she says.

"Why are you hurting yourself?"

Amelia leans back on her chair. "Long story."

"We've got a whole hour."

"It's going to take longer than an hour."

"We'll resume next week. Nothing is rushing us."

"Okay, my girlfriend dumped me..."

"And?"

"The scratching is a way to deal with the pain—it helps me cope."

Dr Keener writes this down. "Self-mutilation is normally a sign of something much more serious. When did you start hurting yourself?"

"In secondary school."

"Do you know why you began to hurt yourself?"

"No, I'm not sure. After my parents separated. By chance, I guess. I liked the way in made me feel. I still do."

"Do you scratch yourself anywhere else?"

Silence for a few seconds.

"My legs," she says.

"Can I see?"

"Why?"

"To confirm it for my report."

They stare at each other for a few seconds.

She says, "I don't have to show you—I don't even like you. I am here because I'm being forced to be here."

Amelia stands up.

"Please, sit down—we're not done yet."

"Can't you just give me my prescription like you normally do?"

"I can't do that anymore."

She walks to the door and says, "Okay, fine—go fuck

yourself!"

Dr Keener seems a little shocked. He is about to respond, but Amelia opens the door and walks out of the consultation room.

Amelia is standing on the other side of a street of the building where Jasmine lives. It's almost dark, and she is wearing her grey hoodie and pair of sunglasses, looking somewhat suspicious. There is no one around her, other than the usual traffic at that time of the day. It's not a main street, so cars only drive past every minute or so. It's a little too warm to wear a hoodie, but there is no one around, so she's not really concerned, even though she should be.

Amelia stares at one of the windows of the apartment. She found the address in the online directory, and it is just as well Jasmine choose to keep a landline.

A young woman goes into the building. She has dark hair down to her back and is slim. She looks early-to-mid twenties. She wears a summer, blue, cotton dress with yellow flower motifs printed on it. Her arse is firm and rounded, and it's obvious she looks after herself.

She closes the wood-and-glass door of the lobby and goes up the stairs to the second floor, where Jasmine lives.

Not long after the woman has gone in, a light in one of the rooms of the apartment is turned on.

Jasmine and the woman appear at the window and kiss. It's like a horrible film cliché.

Amelia's stomach churns.

I'm going to kill the bitch!

Back at the apartment, Amelia is scratching herself again. She's all worked up from having seen Jasmine kissing another woman.

This time the scratching just won't do.

She cuts deeper until she draws blood.

Suddenly she feels relieved. It's exactly what she needs. Physical pain to let her overcome emotional pain.

When she rinses the cut under the tap, it's deeper than she intended, and the bleeding won't stop. For a moment she wonders if she's going to need stitches, but after applying a tight bandage and an icepack she got from the kitchen freezer, the bleeding seems to have stopped.

She spends the rest of the evening lying in bed and going through photos of Jasmine.

Who is this woman? Did she meet Jasmine while we were still together? Is this why Jasmine dumped me?

Amelia hardly sleeps during the night.

She needs to know.

Amelia is waiting in front of Jasmine's apartment. She is dressed again with a hoodie and sunglasses.

She waits a good hour before the young woman she saw the other day comes out of the building. Her face is a little more distinguishable now. It's day time, and sunlight is strong enough to make out her features even from a distance. She has an oblong face with long eyes lashes and dark eyes—probably Spanish or Italian, but it's hard to tell.

Amelia walks up to her and grabs her by the arm.

"Who are you?" Amelia says.

"Excuse-me?" The young woman pulls her arm back.

"Who the *fuck* are you?"

The young woman looks scared now. "You're crazy. I don't know what you want from me."

Amelia grabs the woman's arm again and tightens her grip. "Do you fuck her?"

"What?"

"Do you *fuck* her?"

The young woman pulls her arm back. She takes her cell phone from her bag. "If you don't let go of me, I'm going to call the police."

Amelia slaps her in the face. "Bitch!"

Amelia walks away.

The young woman looks totally shocked and rubs the side of her face where she got slapped.

Back in the kitchen of her apartment, Amelia is in front of her notebook. The notebook is turned on, but she is not doing any work.

Her cell phone is next to the computer.

She picks up the phone, looks up the contact numbers and stops when she gets to the name *Jasmine*.

She presses the dial button.

She waits.

"Hello?" Jasmine says.

Amelia doesn't reply.

"Hello? Amelia?"

Amelia says nothing.

"Amelia, listen, you're seriously starting to give me the shits! You're a crazy bitch, you know?"

Amelia ends the call and places the phone back on the table-top.

Amelia is sorting through some laundry and places dirty clothes in the washing machine. She comes across a yellow tee-shirt Jasmine used to wear. She brings it up to her face and takes a deep breath—it *reeks* of Jasmine. She leaves the laundry with the tee-shirt.

She goes to the kitchen. She places the tee-shirt on the kitchen table. She takes a scissors from the kitchen drawer, goes back to the table and cuts the tee-shirt into pieces, first quietly and then into a frenzy, tearing it with her hands.

Amelia is floating on the surface of the ocean. She stands still like for a little while.

The water is flat, and the sun is straight in her face. She

closes her eyes, the sun rays like fingers on her face. Then she goes under.

CHAPTER NINE

Amelia is sitting opposite Dr Keener.

"You are going to have to accept she's not coming back," Dr Keener says.

Amelia states at him for an uncomfortable amount of time.

"She'll be back," she finally says.

"How can you be sure?"

"Because she's in love with me."

"Did she say that?"

"I know she's in love with me."

Dr Keener takes notes. "Have you considered she might never come back?"

"She'll be back."

"You're living in denial, and you won't make progress if you don't learn to accept the truth."

Amelia stares at him for a few seconds. She starts playing with her hair. "You have no idea what you're talking about."

"We're not here to talk about me."

"I don't even like you."

"You don't have to like me—you only have to talk to me."

Amelia says nothing, just stares at him, like a sulking teenager.

Dr Keener checks his watch.

"Okay, we're done for today," he says.

"Good." She stands from her chair. "Can I have my prescription?"

"Only if you come back next Wednesday."

"I'll be here."

Dr Keener writes the prescription and hands it over the desk.

Amelia takes it. "Are these sessions going to go on for much longer?"

"For as long as it takes."

"For fuck's sake!" she says under her breath.

She leaves the room.

Amelia is lying on the floor of the lounge room. The sun covers her face like a white sheet. There is traffic outside, and the air is warm—a typical spring day.

There's a knock on the front door.

"Come in, it's open!" she yells out.

She can hear the door being open and shut.

In the doorway of the lounge room appears Stéphanie, the girl she danced with at the party. She is wearing jeans and a red-and-white chequered shirt.

"What are you doing?" she asks.

Amelia doesn't reply. She stares at the ceiling—the alcohol and pills she has taken all morning working effectively to dull her senses.

Stéphanie steps up next to her and kneels down. "You know she's not coming back—you have to accept it."

"Not true."

"She's not coming back."

Amelia gives up arguing. No one understands what she's going through—they've never been in love; they don't know what love is.

"Can I get you something?" Stéphanie asks.

"A gun."

"Ha, ha, very funny—seriously, do you want a coffee?"

Stéphanie notices the scratches on Amelia's arm. She takes the arm and looks at the scar.

Amelia doesn't react, numb like a doll.

"Shit, you're still scratching yourself—you should really stop."

"It makes me feel better."

"I know, but there are other ways to cope with life."

Amelia pulls her arm back towards her. "Leave me alone, please."

"You asked me to come over?"

"Well, now I want you to go."

Stéphanie looks somewhat annoyed, almost angry. "It's taken me one hour to get here—the traffic was horrendous; you should be a little more considerate."

"Please!"

Stéphanie stands up. "Okay, fine, but just so you know—she's not coming back"

"Please, go."

"Fine."

Stéphanie storms out of the room.

She slams shut the front door of the apartment.

Amelia stays lying on the floor.

She cries in little spasms.

In the kitchen of her apartment, Amelia is at her notebook. She is typing away. She manages to get into Jasmine's Facebook account. The password was a combination of her new street number and address.

Once in there, she deletes all her friends.

After she's done, she deletes the account.

Amelia is sitting in the toilet, her white panties down to her ankles. She has her cell phone with her. She is texting Jasmine:

GO FUCK YOURSELF!

Amelia is standing opposite Jasmine's apart-ment.

She waits a bit and looks out for movement through the windows. She is wearing her grey hoodie and dark shades.

She crosses the street and removes her house keys from her bag. She walks past a red convertible and scratches the duco form one side to the other. The metal-to-metal screech soothes her anger.

When she's done, she walks off.

Amelia is lying on her bed with her cell phone. She rings up Jasmine.

"Yes?" Jasmine says.

"It's me."

"Christ, did you scratch my car?"

"I want you back."

"Are you nuts?"

"I'll change, you'll see. Forgive me, please come back. I'll pay for the car damage."

"Leave me alone, okay? It's over."

"Jasmine, please—we can't end it this way."

"Never call me again, you understand?"

Jasmine hangs up on her.

Amelia stares at the phone in disbelief.

She doubles up on the bed, curls up and sobs.

CHAPTER TEN

Amelia is sitting opposite Dr Keener. She looks really bad—no make-up, unkempt hair, badly dressed with tracksuit pants and a white, stained tee-shirt. She is tired and hasn't had much sleep for the past week.

Through the office window, she can see the blue sky. She should be out there enjoying life, but it's become too difficult to even breathe.

But it's time to face reality.

"She's not coming back," she says.

Dr Keener stares at her for a few seconds, obviously trying to figure out if she's telling the truth. "It's great you've accepted it. It's a giant step forward," Dr Keener says. He looks happy today, almost as if he is enjoying seeing other people torturing themselves.

What kind of person wants to listen to other people's shit all day long?

"It's my fault," Amelia says. "I hurt her. I lied to her, and I hurt her."

This time Dr Keener looks a little lost for words. He hesitates for a few seconds. "It's never one person's fault."

"I hurt her, and it's the reason she left."

"Do you think you could have done things differently?"

"I don't know. I was angry all the time. I should have told her what was going on in my head."

Amelia looks like she is about to pass out. She is moving from side-to-side on her chair.

Dr Keener says, "You don't look so good. Do you want to end the session now and go home?"

Amelia looks lost, as if she hasn't heard what he'd just said. "Amelia?"

"Uh, yes? Yes, I would like to go home."

"Okay, we're done for today. Let me write you a prescription for Xanax—it's going to make you feel better."

Amelia doesn't reply.

Dr Keener writes the prescription and hands it over to Amelia. She pockets it and stands from her chair.

She walks to the exit.

"Don't forget next Wednesday," Dr Keener says loudly.

Amelia doesn't reply and leaves the room.

Stéphanie is in the kitchen with Amelia. They are sitting at the table.

Amelia looks really pale and sick. She is wearing only a white shirt and pink panties.

Stéphanie says, "You don't look well at all—you need to do something."

"It's these bloody tablets the doctor gave me."

"Stop taking them then."

Amelia doesn't reply. She looks as if she's lost in a trance. "I should have loved her more."

"You're still on about Jasmine? Seriously, you have to let it go."

Amelia now looks at Stéphanie. "What can I do to get her to come back? What would you do?"

"I would let it go."

"Why doesn't she love me anymore?"

74

"Amelia, come on..."

"Why doesn't anyone love me?"

Amelia stands from her chair and goes to the fridge. She opens the freezer compartment and removes a bottle of vodka.

"What are you doing?" Stéphanie says. "It's ten in the morning!"

Amelia unscrews the cap and takes a mouthful.

Stéphanie stands from her chair and goes to where Amelia is. "My god, you're going to kill yourself." Stéphanie grabs the bottle from Amelia's hands. "You're not the first person in the world who got dumped."

Amelia tries to grab the bottle back. "Give it to me—please!"

Stéphanie empties the contents of the bottle in the sink.

Amelia is shocked. "Do you have any idea how much a bottle of Vodka costs?"

"Ah, no, no idea."

Stéphanie tosses the empty bottle to the side.

Then, she grabs Amelia by the shoulders. "You need help!"

Amelia goes back to the chair and sits, defeated. "I'm sick of everything."

Stéphanie goes and sits next to her. She grabs her hand. "You've broke up—it's normal."

"I never thought it would be this difficult."

Stéphanie squeezes Amelia's hand and gives her a side hug.

Amelia is lying naked on the kitchen floor of her apartment—numb.

The fridge door is open. Dishes are not washed. Garbage is tossed around. The kitchen is pretty much a mess.

For the next few days, Amelia stays in bed. Her room is a total mess of unwashed clothes, newspapers, magazines and junk. She hasn't cleaned for a while. She only gets up to go to the bathroom or grab something from the fridge. But there is not much food in there, and she is mostly surviving on milk and booze.

Amelia is sitting at the kitchen table in the dark. She is not doing anything.

Amelia is scratching herself. She suddenly stops, drops the nail file and cries.

Amelia is lying on the floor in the kitchen.
    She seems out of it.
    The door bell rings.
    She ignores it.
    The door bell rings again.
    She gets up slowly and struggles to get to the door. She picks up the security phone.
    "Yes?" she says.
    "It's me, you're going to let me in?"
    Her father. She really doesn't feel like seeing him. She waits a few seconds.
    "Amelia, it's dad, are you going to let me in?"
    "Okay, come up."
    She presses the entry button for the building and hangs up the phone.
    She unlocks the front door and leaves it ajar.
    Not waiting, she returns to the kitchen.
    Fabien walks in the kitchen. He wears a green shirt and a pair of jeans. He has a shocked expression when seeing the mess around him. He doesn't dare to sit, but she stands a metre from the table.
    "What's going on here?" he says.
    "Nothing."
    "I can see something is going on." Hen looks at the mess around him. "Not very clean at your place."

"I don't care."

"And Jasmine is not back yet?"

"We broke up."

"Really—just now?"

"Two months ago."

Fabien seems confused. He tries to make eye-contact with his daughter, but she avoids it. "But, you told me—"

"I know—I lied."

"Ah!"

She looks at him almost angry. "What do you want?"

Fabien approaches the table and stands next to her, this time more confident and assertive. "Why are you being rude to me?"

"Listen, right now I just want everyone to leave me alone, you understand?"

He is angry now. "I'm getting tired of this. To date I have been nothing but kind to you—and maybe that's the problem."

Amelia is surprised by his anger. She rolls her eyes, and turns away from him. "Get lost."

"Don't talk to me that way."

"You're fuckin' annoying."

Fabien moves closer to her.

Amelia stands from her chair and eyeballs him. "And what? You're going to hit me now? Is that what happened with mum?"

"You little—"

"Little what?"

"Little..."

"...bitch? Is that it?"

Fabien holds back from hitting her.

Amelia says, "Well, listen, the girl you saw in the hallway the other day, I fuck her—and she's not the only one. I fucked three different girls every week. Does it turn you on?"

Fabien seems a little shocked, but he picks up quickly. "Oh, you know, I'm not surprised—you're just like your mother."

"Ah, men—you are all the same. Fifteen or fifty years old, all a bunch of fuckin' arseholes, fuckin' pigs. That's why I like girls better."

This time Fabien loses it and slaps her in the face.

Amelia is shocked.

She storms out of the kitchen.

Fabien sands there, somewhat stupefied by what he has done.

Amelia slams the door of her bedroom.

"Amelia!" He goes after her.

Amelia is lying on her bed, her face covered in tears.

There's a knock on the door.

"Amelia!"

The bedroom door is pushed open.

Fabien walks in, an embarrassed and panicked look etched on his face. "Amelia, I'm sorry..."

Amelia continues to cry and avoids eye contact with her father.

Fabien approaches the bed and sits on the edge.

"I'm sorry—I don't know what took over me..."

Amelia continues to ignore him.

He moves forth and grabs her hand. "Forgive me—I can't stand seeing you so sad."

She is still sobbing.

"Forgive me..."

Amelia turns to face him. "I can't do this anymore, daddy..."

He moves towards her, and she sits up and falls into his arms in a hug.

She says, "I love her so much—I can't live without her."

"Amelia, my poor little girl—you're breaking my heart."

"I don't know what to do anymore. I'm sick of everything." She begins to sob again.

Fabien holds her tight. "Don't worry—everything will work itself out."

She stays in his arms and cries in silence.

He strokes her hair and she rests her head against his chest. "You have to be strong in life—don't let yourself go."

She says nothing and just stays in his arms.

I'm never going to be strong enough.

CHAPTER ELEVEN

Amelia takes all the prescription vials and empties the contents in the toilet.

She then reaches in the cabinet, removes a bag of heroin and empties it in the toilet.

She flushes.

She spends the rest of the day cleaning her apartment.

When done, she opens the freezer, removes a bottle of vodka and empties the contents in the sink. She tosses the bottle in the bin. She removes the garbage bag from the bin and takes it downstairs to the wheelie bin assigned to her apartment number.

When she returns to the apartment, she cleans her bedroom. She takes all the photos of Jasmine and puts them in a cardboard box. She also takes whatever remaining clothes there are that belong to Jasmine and puts them in the same box.

Amelia is standing on the other side of the road of Jasmine's apartment. She is holding the cardboard box she filled with her clothes and photos. She is wearing her grey hoodie and shades.

It's a beautiful day. The sky is blue, the air warm and she hears birds singing amongst the foliage of the elms surrounding her.

She crosses the road.

She drops the box at the front door and pushes the buzzer.

A woman answers. "Yes?"

"There's a package for Jasmine. I am leaving it by the door."

Amelia doesn't wait for a reply and races back across the street.

She hides behind a tree and looks on.

Jasmine's girlfriend opens the front door of the apartment It's the girl she slapped in the face. She wears a short, red dress and looks very alluring. She sees the box on the floor. She looks around, but doesn't notice Amelia hiding behind the tree.

Jasmine's girlfriend kneels down and checks the contents of the box. She closes the box again and stands up with the box in her hands. She looks around once more, and then she enters the building with the box.

Satisfied, Amelia walks off.

The kitchen is very clean for the first time in weeks.

The table is set for two.

Amelia places a dish on the table.

There is a knock on the front door.

Amelia leaves the kitchen.

She comes back with Stéphanie.

Stéphanie looks around. "Wow, it's super clean here—it must have taken you ages."

She lies. "My father helped me."

Stéphanie sits at the table.

Amelia does the same.

Stéphanie says, "You look great—like you're much better."

"One day at a time, as they say."

"I'm really happy to see you like this."

Amelia smiles. "You can't live in the past forever."

"True."

Amelia looks at all the food on the table—green salad with onion rings and tomatoes, chicken, mash potatoes, beans, bread. "Okay, what would you like?"

Stéphanie looks at the food and tries to decide. "A bit of everything."

"Okay."

Amelia fills up Stéphanie's plate.

Stéphanie says, "You don't have any news from Jasmine?"

"Ah, no."

"Did you hear how her girlfriend dumped her?"

Amelia seems a little surprised. "Tell me..."

"Not really sure—but apparently she found some photos of you and Jasmine in Jasmine's side drawer, and they argued, and they split."

Amelia is a little shocked. She stares at Stéphanie.

"You okay?" Stéphanie says.

No reply.

"Amelia?"

Amelia snaps out of it. "Ah, no...I mean yes, I'm fine."

Amelia smiles and eats her food.

That same night Amelia is sitting on her bed, starring at the empty space.

Warm tears roll down her face.

She grabs her pillow and hugs it.

She opens a drawer, and there she finds a prescription vial with pills in it she forgot to throw out. She looks at it for a few seconds, unscrews the top, takes a couple of pills and swallows them dry without water.

When done, she throws the vial across the room.

Amelia is standing opposite Jasmine's apartment—hoodie and

shades.

She crosses the street and walks up to the front door of the building.

She presses Jasmine's apartment buzzer.

A few seconds.

"Yes?" Jasmine says.

Amelia is about to reply, her mouth half open, but then she says nothing. She stares at the rows of buzzers instead.

"Martine? Is that you?" Jasmine asks.

Amelia stands in front of the door for a few more seconds and then walks away down the street.

Jasmine's voice calls out again. "Martine!?"

At the kitchen table of her apartment, Amelia is typing on her notebook. She looks a little better than the previous day— casually dressed with denim shorts and a white tee-shirt, but clean and refreshed.

There's a knock on the door.

She looks up, a little surprised, clearly not expecting anyone.

She stands from the chair and leaves the kitchen.

She walks down the hallway and opens the front door.

Yvette walks in without saying a word. She pushes Amelia gently against the wall of the hallway and kisses her.

Amelia takes her kiss in.

They pull back.

"Did you get my message?" Amelia says.

Yvette smiles. "Of course, why else would I be here?"

Yvette kisses her again and pulls back. She says, "Damn, you're driving me insane."

Amelia smiles back.

She takes Yvette's hand and leads her to the bedroom.

They enter the bedroom.

They make love. Not just sex, but love. It's the first time since she made love to Jasmine that she's made love to someone else.

When they are done, they fall back on the bed. She feels like one with Yvette.

Yvette says, "I don't think it's really going to work between us."

Amelia nods. "No big deal—I'm not asking for anything."

"Ah, all right then." Yvette seems disappointed Amelia is not arguing the point. She pushes her red hair away from her face. "But it doesn't mean we shouldn't try."

"Let's see how we go."

Amelia snuggles herself against Yvette.

She just wants life to slow down for a while.

CHAPTER TWELVE

Amelia is sitting opposite Dr Keener. She looks confident and self-assured.

"You look much better," Dr Keener says.

"Thanks."

"Is there something in particular you would like to talk about today?"

"Okay, I know I'm going to have to talk—I don't think I need another prescription."

"And why not?"

"I feel great."

Dr Keener scribbles in his note-pad. "It's great to be confident, but it's up to me to eva-luate if you need another prescription or not."

"Fine—what do you want to know?"

"Are you sleeping well?"

"Yes."

"Eating well?"

"Yes."

"Are you still drinking?"

"I haven't touched a drop in three weeks."

Dr Keener writes all this down. "Well, I'm impressed. But

how do I know you're not telling me what I want to hear?"

"You don't. You have to trust me in the same way I have to trust you."

Dr Keener smiles, and he very rarely smiles during those sessions. "You're right." He writes down more notes and closes the note-pad. "Well, I don't think we are going to need to see each other again—unless you feel you need to see me again?"

"No, I'm good now. It's going to be fine."

"Have you found another job?"

"I've decided to go back to study."

"Very good. What field?"

"Law."

Dr Keener smiles.

Amelia stands from her chair.

Dr Keener extends his hand. "Good luck, young woman."

They shake hands.

Amelia says, "I need to apologise."

"No, you don't."

"I was nasty with you. It wasn't you I hated—it was myself."

"Not an issue—and anyway, I didn't believe you."

"My apologies, either way."

"Thank you."

"Well, farewell, I hope..."

Amelia turns around and leaves the room.

Amelia walks out of the university grounds. It's overcast, but the air is warm like maple syrup. Students are buzzing around, like people on holidays. They have all their lives in front of them, but few know what to do with it.

Yvette joins her.

They kiss.

"I missed you," Yvette says.

"I missed you, too."

They walk hand-in-hand in the street.

Yvette is asleep.

The room is dark with just enough light from the street lamps outside to make-out the shadows of the furniture. It smells of perfume and sex from the previous night.

Quietly, Amelia steps from the bed and leaves the bedroom for the bathroom.

She opens the bathroom cabinet. She re-moves a nail file. She sits on the edge of the bathtub and begins scratching her arm.

The relief is instantaneous.

ALSO BY LAURENT BOULANGER

ADDICTION

"Today is the day Danielle is going to find out her sister is a complete bitch." Danielle lives a quiet life until she arrives from work one day, and her young sister Sarah is wrapped around naked with Danielle's boyfriend on her couch. Straight out of rehab, Sarah wants to re-start her life but goes all the wrong way about it. Slowly she slides back into addiction and effects everyone around her. Danielle must choose to help Sarah and let her go forever.

NOW AVAILABLE IN PAPERBACK
AND EBOOKS WORLDWIDE

LAKE OZARK PRESS
MISSOURI, USA

ALSO BY LAURENT BOULANGER

THE RESEARCH

Nathan is convinced his partner Lucia is cheating on him; Lucia is having an affair with Lorenzo, a man half her age; Lorenzo is sleeping with his friend, Tom; Tom is kicked out of home and seduces Walter to get free shelter; Walter is no longer in love with Marilyn; Marilyn cannot accept rejection. Six interconnected people are interviewed about their most intimate secrets and opinions of love for a university research project. Everything is recorded on camera. Suspicion about the research's underlying intentions for the recordings is aroused when one of the lovers commits suicide and Lucia becomes pregnant. With the recordings acting as a catalyst, the lovers question whether the information they first gave freely is now controlling them.

NOW AVAILABLE IN PAPERBACK
AND EBOOKS WORLDWIDE

LAKE OZARK PRESS
MISSOURI, USA

ALSO BY LAURENT BOULANGER

THE GIRL FROM FRANCE

WINNER 2014 PARIS BOOK FESTIVAL AWARDS - #1 EBOOK,
WORLDWIDE, ALL CATEGORIES

WINNER 2014 GOLD #1 GLOBAL EBOOK AWARDS FOR BEST
MULTICULTURAL LITERATURE FICTION

In the cold winter of Strasbourg, a medieval town in the North-East of France, 11-year-old Clotilde is living a quiet existence with her frail father, a Catholic priest. To the world outside, she is an adopted child—in reality, she is the bastard child of a sinful relationship. In the loneliness of her existence, she daydreams of literature and hot summers in Provence. She self-destructs with wine, cigarettes and shaving blades. Her last chance for a normal life is to migrate to Australia and live with her mother who abandoned her at birth. She is forced into a strange land where nobody understands her and where her precocious attitude leads her to the shocking truth about her existence.

NOW AVAILABLE IN PAPERBACK
AND EBOOKS WORLDWIDE

LAKE OZARK PRESS
MISSOURI, USA

ALSO BY LAURENT BOULANGER

A GUIDE FOR THE NEW NOVELIST

In this small, but comprehensive, volume, Dr Laurent Boulanger shares his wisdom of years of combined creative writing knowledge for the new novelist. He goes through the various aspects of setting yourself up as a novelist, including what genre to write in, career advice, traditional vs new publishing opportunities, not giving up, time management, and learning the craft. It includes his award-winning short story 'My Father's Last Breath'.

NOW AVAILABLE IN PAPERBACK
AND EBOOKS WORLDWIDE

LAKE OZARK PRESS
MISSOURI, USA

ALSO BY LAURENT BOULANGER

BETTER DEAD THAN NEVER

Patricia Lunn takes on a hopeless case after an old friend from her days in uniform asks her to dig into a supposedly wrong conviction of a serial rapist turned killer. But as she knocks at the doors of the city's most influential people, someone wants her dead before she finds out the truth. She uncovers a world filled with police corruption, racism, sexual debauchery and a killer who will do anything to protect his identity...including putting a contract on her head.

NOW AVAILABLE IN PAPERBACK
AND EBOOKS WORLDWIDE

LAKE OZARK PRESS
MISSOURI, USA

www.ingramcontent.com/pod-product-compliance
Lightning Source LLC
Chambersburg PA
CBHW030537180626
46810CB00005B/1905